DELIVER ME FROM NOWHERE

DELIVER ME
FROM NOWHERE

TENNESSEE JONES

SOFT SKULL PRESS
BROOKLYN, NY 2005

Published by Soft Skull Press
71 Bond Street
Brooklyn, NY 11217
www.softskull.com

Distributed by Publishers Group West
www.pgw.com | 1.800.388.3123

Printed in Canada

Cataloging in Publication data for this title available from
the Library of Congress.

For Ammi Emergency
and
Sera Bilezikian (1978–2001)

Forever and ever, Amen.

CONTENTS

NEBRASKA

I was standing on my front lawn the first time I saw him. He was walking up the street, dressed in blue jeans and a denim jacket. It was sunny that day and something about the way the denim looked against the blue of the sky made me notice him. It was late afternoon, closing in on evening. All of the colors were so bright I almost didn't feel solid on the earth as I twirled my baton. It flew across my hands in all the ways I could remember from when I was little. I was waiting for my daddy to call me to dinner.

He slowed down when he passed in front of the yard. "You're real good at that," he said.

"Thank you." Something about the way he looked at me made me feel shy.

"What's your name?"

"Who wants to know?" I asked.

He smiled. "Well, my name's George, if you want to know."

Sweat darkened the hair on his head. The white T-shirt he wore was a little dirty.

"Where'd you learn how to do that?" he asked.

About that time my daddy yelled from inside the house for me to come in. It took my eyes a minute to adjust to the dimness.

"Who the hell was that out in the yard?"

"Just some man, Daddy."

Our town is small. Once when I was little Daddy took me across the state to visit my cousins and there was almost nothing the whole damned way. Sometimes corn and wheat stretched on for miles and miles, brown and gold all the way to the point where it disappeared into the sky. When we got back, Lincoln seemed awfully busy, with people walking out on the sidewalks to jobs and school and wherever else they had to go. For the first day even buying groceries seemed like something special. I guess if you look at it the right way, it always is.

I go to school every day by the same route. I turn left out the door and onto Rosedale. After a few blocks I cut through a nice alleyway that has vines thick with purple grapes in the summertime. They're just about perfect when I go back to school at the end of August. The alley turns out on to Maple Street, and that's the street my school is on.

One day when I came out of the alley George was right there, walking up Maple Street. I nearly ran into him. I didn't even recognize him until he said something to me.

"Hey there. How come you ain't got your baton?"

"Can't carry it around with me all the time," I said. "I gotta go. I'm going to school."

"Well, why don't you let me walk you?"

I looked at him hard for a second. "Depends of whether or not you can give me a good reason for why you want to." Truth was, I couldn't decide if I had a good reason for wanting him not to.

He smiled and the sweat the morning sun had caused made him look kind of beautiful. I noticed the cuffs on the sleeves of his jean jacket were greasy with dirt.

"How about just wantin to, is that reason enough?"

"There's always something behind the wanting and that's what I want to know," I said.

"Is there?" he paused. "I never thought about it like that."

"Oh, yeah?" I asked and started walking towards school. The shadows from the trees that lined the streets moved over both of us as we walked.

"I think you could drive yourself crazy like that, always trying to get to the very first thing. Unless you just pick something to be the beginning, you could go on forever trying to find it. It might not even exist."

"That's a scary thought. How can something be if it never got a start?"

George shrugged. "I guess it just ain't that important. What matters most is what's happening right now."

I nodded and wondered if one of my friend's parents would see us walking together and call my father. I didn't know how old George was, but he looked like he could be ten or fifteen years older than me. And I figured I had a pretty good idea of why he wanted to walk me to school even if he said he didn't.

The red brick of the high school building looked nice in the sun. The lawn was bright green and kids swarmed all over. Somewhere inside a bell rang and the sound carried into the street.

"I gotta go. I'm late," I said.

"When am I gonna see you again?" he yelled. I heard him, but I was already halfway to the big double doors and didn't feel like turning to yell back at him.

I found out a couple of weeks later that he was a trash slinger. I saw him one morning in my favorite alley right before school. He stopped to talk to me even though the man driving the garbage truck glared at him. His pants were greasy down the front and he wore big gloves. He smiled when he saw me walking up, like being elbow deep in trash was nothing to be ashamed of.

"Good morning," he said, grinning like a shark. "I figured I'd see you again soon. Town ain't that big."

"I didn't know you was no trash man," I said, to see if he'd flinch. "What would I do with some garbage man?"

He looked down and smiled. If he hadn't been wearing those filthy gloves he would have grabbed the back of his neck. "I ain't gonna be a trash man forever. This is temporary. You think every place you're in, you're gonna be there forever?"

"I hope I'm not in school forever."

"And you're not gonna be. Bet you're laying some big plans for yourself right now, ain't you?"

I didn't say anything. I looked at the interior slime of the garbage truck.

"George, man, c'mon. We gotta go," the driver yelled.

He jumped up on the back of the truck and held on. He looked at me, squinting in the bright sunlight. "What I want to know is how to get you to make me part of your plans."

I pretended to ignore what he said. "Why wasn't you slinging trash the other morning?"

"Why, I told you. This is temporary. I just started doing this."

I looked at him hard. I didn't really care whether or not he was a garbage man. It didn't make a difference to me like it would to some of the stupid girls I went to school with.

"What don't you come to the park on Clinton at seven o'clock? I might decide not to show up to meet you, though."

George smiled. "All right!" he shouted to the driver and they rumbled off. And that was how things started between us.

*

I never showed him to my daddy. He would have taken one look at him and called him a sonofabitch and ran for his gun. I met him on street corners or in the park instead. There was one bar a friend of his run and he'd let me come in with George. These are the places we spent time together. I never thought to ask him why he didn't have a car.

School let out and we started to see each other more. I saw him during the day after his trash pick-up while my daddy was at work. Finally I started letting him into the house through the back door. The first time we did it was in my bed. I bled a little on the sheets and washed them that afternoon. I was a virgin and the feel of him peeling away from my body was almost unbearable. It was a surprise that someone could get that close and then just leave again. I remember how the summer heat made the dust in the room swim.

Some days it seemed like the scent of us would be so thick that I was sure my father would smell it when he came home. I kept waiting for him to notice that something about me had changed. If he ever did, he never let on. The only time he looked at me sideways was when I put on dinner a little bit late.

I still don't really understand how people fall in love. I just know it happens. I know that sometimes it has a whole lot to do with sex. Or I guess it always has to do with it, whether it's happening or not.

Sometimes when you can't have it it hangs in the air and makes everything mean more than it should.

That summer was different from any other summer. Maybe it was because of sex. I had never considered that my body was so separate from everyone else until I felt the sensation of trying to make that body disappear with someone. There was always a barrier between the two of us, no matter how much we sweated or cursed to knock it down.

Looking back on it, it seems like George was trying hard to get inside my head—like if he asked just the right question, like turning a lock with a key, he would know everything about me. Or maybe I only say this because I was trying so damn hard to get in there myself. Being around George might have even been my way of doing it, looking at the strange reflection of myself in someone I loved.

That summer I realized how big the sky is in Nebraska, bigger maybe than any other place on earth. I wonder sometimes if it's just a big emptiness up there or if there's something else. It's hard to think it's just empty. If it is, what does that make me?

George always said he don't believe in God. Said he ain't got much hope or faith in anything. Laying out in the field one day with his hand in my hair, I asked him what he was living for. "Just this minute. Nothing else you can count on. I'm not laying any big plans. I might die anytime."

I thought this was a peculiar way to think. My daddy was telling me every minute about how I had to make good grades so I could get into a good college and make something out of myself. George acted like he'd never wanted to be anything more than just a man. Maybe that's what made me fall in love with him, the way he didn't let his time belong to any other person or any other place.

The part everyone wants to know about happened the winter after I met George. It was 1958. I didn't see it when he shot my father. I heard the gunshot and then there was George grabbing onto my arm, saying "We got to get out of here. C'mon. Get in the car now." I knew my father must have been dead, but for the life of me, I couldn't make myself feel sorry about it. He was like a specter moving through the house. I don't know if his life meant anything.

The night after George killed my father I learned that driving is a gift. We swallowed up mile after mile. I thought about all the people who had died on wagon trains trying to get across the country. It took them months. We'd end up going almost halfway across in just a few days, dust blowing out from under the wheels.

The fields once we started driving were all frozen over, the gray yellow stubs of corn still standing in them. Everything was silver and yellow, from the big cold clouds to the prairie grass. We rode on a lot of dirt roads that aren't on the map, cutting across the counties and big cornfields. The dirt was hard packed and cold. I prayed it wouldn't snow.

I didn't understand what George meant to do until we pulled up to a service station. A man in grease-darkened pants came around to pump the gas and when it came time to pay, George turned his pockets inside out and smiled at him. When the man put his face in the window and starting yelling at him, George opened the door fast and knocked him down. Cold, dry dust puffed up on his dirty white shirt. George looked down at him for a minute, then took the gun he'd used to kill my father from the backseat and shot the man. I heard him scream as I was looking out at the wide horizon. The smell of gasoline was sharp.

The second time he did it I watched him pull the trigger. We had just crossed over into South Dakota. I felt something in me change. The future receded. It became as dim and unimportant as I had always suspected it might be. But the present lit up in a way it never had before, brighter than the lights of gas stations that appeared on the dark horizon every hour or so when we were driving, brighter than the bars we stopped at once or twice so he could have a beer.

In a roadhouse in eastern Montana he killed everyone in one bar, three men with their cowboy boots hooked on stools and their heavy coats in a pile on the floor, and the bartender. He poured his own beer and sat there and drank it slow, his gun across his lap. The silence in the bar was huge, bigger because their last bits of conversation were still ringing in my head. George finished his beer and then, like always, we got back into the car.

We went into a few places before George's face and name were on the television and radio so much. After that he had to kill anyone who saw us. Before that, the people who waited on us shied away from George like he caused a chill. I felt it like I'd been lying down deep in grass for half the day and was full of warmth from the sun and the ground. The coldness of it didn't touch me.

I started to grow older while we were driving. I don't know exactly how much. Maybe a day or week for each mile. While we were driving, I started to feel something like I imagined religion was supposed to feel like. I almost wanted to clap my hand on his knee and yell, "Hey, George, I think I got religion!" He'd laugh at that, and then he'd ask me what the hell I was talking about. I knew I wouldn't really be able to explain it to him, so I kept my mouth shut.

But if I was going to explain, explain it for myself, I would say that part of driving is that you can go forever having not done anything except move, and that can be enough. Only something did happen rolling around in that car. Something happened to me. I was never young in the same way after that. It wasn't the few years that I spent locked up in a girls' home that did it either. It was those days out riding through emptiness. I read somewhere after I got out that the road can be a holy thing. People try to find things just by moving. I remember his smile, just like chilly sunshine, the kind of cold, thin light that the sun throws off early on a winter morning.

I remember a Bible verse from when I was little. That was the only time we ever went to church, when my mother was still alive. I think that maybe I was too young to have heard it, because it's stuck with me since then and given me bad dreams on occasion. It's from the book of Revelation and it reads something like "God loves the hot and cold, but spews out the lukewarm." It still gives me bad dreams, because it was George that was either ice cold or red hot. I know that I was the lukewarm one.

I'll never stop remembering the countryside we passed through. The light on those days seemed muted and off, like time had been slowed down or speeded up, but I couldn't tell which. It fell across the sand hills and dead trees at an angle that didn't make any sense. We kept driving right through it, past the twisted, rotted farmhouses and slow-blinking cows. A few times we saw police lights flashing red and blue in the darkness and turned off onto one of the unpaved, unnamed roads that mark up the west.

Sometimes there were towns on those roads, awful places with no more than a couple dozen people. They were orange out in all that black land and dark, silvery sky, white houses turned the strangest colors by the winter and that light. Strange to think we could have killed off a whole town and nobody would have known for days. I'm still not sure why he didn't do that. I think something about the desolation must have felt powerful to him, like those people understood part of what he was looking for. That's how I felt, and I didn't want to touch them.

I could never tell when he was going to do it. Maybe he couldn't either. I never felt scared of what he might do to me, but I was scared of talking to him about it.

"What was it about that man back there?" I asked.

A shrug. A cigarette chucked out the window. "I don't think I need a reason for that. He was doing what he does and here I am doing what I do." And then he wouldn't talk past that.

The way he wouldn't talk sometimes made me angry so I made up my own reasons after that. I couldn't drive so I just looked at everything. I looked even when it seemed like there was nothing to look at. There were stories on stories in those little towns we passed, and they spread out like ripples in water. After a while I started to pick out shapes in the darkness and even in the daylight we drove through. Some of the things I saw were etched in light and others were like pieces of black felt cut out and pasted onto the night. I saw the darkness that lies like slivers in some people's hearts and the dark that eats some people up whole.

Those dark shapes started to get to me after awhile. They started making me look at my own heart. I wondered how much that was in there was actually my own. I wondered where all the dark things came from; I was surprised by how much there was. I know not everyone would have gone off with George the way I did, but I had to see what happened. I had to see what would open up inside of me.

The mountains that rose up between Montana and Wyoming terrified me. Wyoming is where they finally caught us. I'd never seen mountains before, but I knew what they were. One of my little cousins cried for days when his momma took him out East. He was terrified of the old, worn Appalachians. The Rockies looked like monsters out there, like an awful darkness the land had been cursed with.

Most people know what happened afterwards. Some people know more than others, like the cops that took care of George and looked the other way because he gave them a button off his jacket or an autograph. The cops acted like he was some kind of hero when they finally caught him. He was still wearing blue jeans and a T-shirt, just like the first time I met him. They wanted to get near him, to have some kind of proof that they had been close to him. And then there were all the stories about both of us. The movies that didn't have anything to do with what had happened but everything to do with making a story. I realized that people don't really care about what something is about sometimes, as long as it's a good story. As long as it's a good story, then they'll make whatever meaning they need from it come out of it.

I still wonder if he expected to make it through. It was like he wanted to turn the lights on full blast before going instead of just fading off into the darkness. Maybe he thought if he lived long enough he'd start to get afraid of dying. I think about his last moments sometimes, but I don't really know what it is I'm thinking about. I guess they were awful to watch, his arms and legs held down by leather straps.

I think I'm surprised to still be here. They let me go after a while. I was in a mental hospital for a few weeks and then a girls' detention center. They figured George had fooled me and I never pulled the trigger on any of those people. I didn't pull the trigger, but I wonder if just sitting there and watching it happen is even worse.

The last thing I remember about our ride is the sky in Montana. The sky before those horrible mountains came up in front of it was the biggest sky I'd ever seen. Bigger than Nebraska, so big that you could go crazy just from looking at it. You want to fill your chest up with it, but the size of it will stretch you out, make you realize how empty you really are. I looked up into that void while we were driving, looked up into it when we'd stop the car on the side of the road, looked at it in the cold sun, looked at it sparkling with the hard shapes of stars, and I recognized it as my own heart.

ATLANTIC CITY

The day Frank and Eliza arrived in Atlantic City they watched a woman drive a motorcycle across a tightrope that had been strung above the pier. She was dressed in a daredevil outfit decorated with red, white, and blue stars. A woman in a matching leotard hung from a trapeze attached the bottom of the motorcycle. They roared up the slanted tightrope, and then idled backwards over and over again. The woman driving raised her hand to wave while the woman below twirled and twisted.

They discovered the tightrope act by accident. The bus had let them off near the boardwalk, and they wandered onto the pier. World-famous, the sign said. A song neither of them recognized came from the loudspeakers. *Here comes Johnny Yen again/with liquor and drugs/liquor and drugs.* Little kids turned their heads up to watch the two women go across, and the ocean gave off a cool that said summer is almost gone. Frank and Eliza wondered why they had waited so long to come here.

The boardwalk was very crowded and they were glad they had only a few bags. Men lined up by wide rickshaw things called to people, but Frank didn't see how they could maneuver though all the people who crowded the boardwalk. Most of them spoke in heavy accents he had never heard before. They were white, but not the kind of white he was used to. *Off white*, he joked to himself.

They saw a fat older woman sitting on the ledge of one of the plate glass windows of the Showboat Casino. Her feet were planted squarely on the planks of the boardwalk and she blinked out towards the beach, a smear of yellow mustard at the edge of her lower lip. Her cheeks were rouged bright pink and she wore fuchsia pants and a lemon yellow shirt. Her hair was greasy white platinum, like smoke from a green fire.

Eliza felt a tightening when she saw the woman, disgust a thin, sharp necklace around her neck. Frank wondered if anyone had ever loved that woman, and instead imagined Eliza pulling her stockings over her slim legs, her arches flexed, fingers smoothing as she went up. There was the curve of her thigh up under her dress and he knew it would be there as it always had been, smooth and warm to the touch of his hand. Smooth and warm whether his hand touched her or not.

Their motel was a cheap one near an abandoned school that looked like the halls might be lined with crypts. The school was built with large stones, and the half-hearted chain link fence that surrounded it opened up onto lots resplendent with weeds, broken glass, and torn up pavement. The shadows beneath the fire escapes were very long and dark by the time they made it back to their room that night.

They had their good clothes on from the bus ride. They were even nicer than what people would call Sunday clothes out in the country, where they were from. Eliza hated the expression. The dress was one that had always been one of her favorites, but she had had to lose weight to be able to fit into it again. Frank pulled on a heavy, black suit jacket and a shirt that was blinding white except for a ring of yellow around the neck. He had rarely worn it in the time he had owned it. His hair gleamed with the expensive grease he used only on special occasions. He packed it in the small black bag he took with him.

The day before getting on the bus they had gone to the bank together and closed out their accounts. All the money they had in the world was in the bottom of each of their bags, in special panels Eliza had sewn into them. Each of them had packed lightly, and they both enjoyed the feeling of covering up such a big secret.

Neither of them had taken a long bus ride before. Eliza walked ahead of him and chose their seats carefully. After they had placed their bigger bags on the racks above them, she settled down and looked out the window. The streets of her hometown looked very different from the high bus window.

Frank had never seen the ocean before. He leaned his head back and tried to imagine the feel of it against his ankles. *How many things can a person never do in his life?* Eliza reached over to clasp his hand, and he noticed that some of the people climbing on the bus smiled at them. Her wrist was pale and small against the brushed black of his suit coat.

In Pennsylvania the bus turned off the interstate and stopped in a half dozen former mining towns. The few people who got on in those towns had a similar look to them, tough foreheads and wide cheeks and skin that was somehow pale and ruddy at once. The land was hilly, and many of the hills were old piles of coal slag that trees and brush had taken root on. People got on and off, and after a while the rhythm of it lulled Frank to sleep.

In the motel room they took their clothes off in the dark and slid between the crisp white sheets. The sink leaked quietly from the bathroom, and they fell into an exhausted sleep, with the sound working its way into their dreams.

The next day they went into the casinos for the first time. The noise was church cacophony when they entered. Hundreds of slot machines sat side by side in rows on the thick purple carpet. Each had its own sounds that filled each part of the huge room and, midway to the ceiling, blended into one harmony. It crystallized around Frank and Eliza as the stood on the rising escalator before it crashed into noise again.

"Let's go down there now, babe," he said to Eliza, his hand on her arm. They rode to the top and then rode down. There was an entire section of slots occupied by old ladies with white hair and buckets of nickels at their feet. They talked as they played, spinning the reels again and again. They seemed sad to Eliza, and she looked quickly away. On the floor, the golden harmony was reduced to its small parts. She wanted to go to the card tables, where she could place big bets.

Still, the noise carried them. Cocktail waitresses brushed against them with trays of watered down drinks in plastic cups. Frank wondered what the place would be like with no people and saw flashes of the big empty halls he had once swept at night. He realized the casino was never empty, and couldn't even imagine what it would be like if it was. He remembered how he had felt cleaning the empty textile factory at night after the day shift had clocked out.

The old ladies sent a chill through Eliza. She adjusted her skirt as she walked by. She could even smell them, the powdery scent of something that doesn't get used anymore. The heels of her black shoes sank into the thick carpet, and she imagined she was stabbing the floor as she walked by them.

"Should we do the tables or the slots?" she asked.

"Tables got bigger bets."

"Mmmm-hmmm." She looked at him.

"We don't want to lose it all at once," he said.

"Frank, we're not gonna lose or we wouldn't be here."

"Do you think we have enough?"

Eliza took him by the arm. "We have to have enough, honey. Why don't you try the slots and I'll see how the tables are."

She pushed him down in front of one of the nickel slots and he felt confused. He stared at the machine after she walked off and realized he needed to exchange his dollars. He looked around and saw two signs: Boardwalk Redemption and Self Redemption.

On his way back with the bucket of nickels he noticed the way most people were dressed: khaki pants or jeans and white shirts and sneakers. He took off his suit jacket and rolled up the sleeves of his white shirt. He let the nickel go in the slot and then pulled the lever down. His heart skipped when the pieces of fruit and numbers didn't line up. He put another nickel to the slot and let it go. He did this until his arm became tired and he realized he could just push a button in front of him to get the reels to spin.

He sat at the machine for hours; he won his money back again and again, but didn't hit anything big. He found an easy place between nickel-to-machine and spinning the reels. It was like digging a tunnel with a teaspoon. A group of old ladies walked behind him and laughed loudly. He took a moment to watch and wondered if Eliza would ever look as they did. Would he still be able to love her?

The slot machines reminded him of the old time clock they used to punch. You'd stick your card in and pull down the lever so it'd make an imprint and that was your mark for the night. He remembered the nights they had passed part of their shift at Fernback's by working themselves hard for the first half, meeting up at lunch, and then going into one of the locked offices that Eliza cleaned. He washed his hands, his big hard knuckles, carefully before they went in there. He did this gingerly, but he was never too careful with her. She liked to lay with her back on the hard floor, her hair still in the rag she did it up with when she worked. He clapped his big clean hands over her mouth to keep her from screaming too loudly, and their breath echoed off the empty walls.

Eliza walked through the ringing machines toward the card tables. Some were empty, the dealers in vests looking bored, and some were jammed with both players and spectators. The noise made Eliza's heart beat faster, and she smiled her best smile as she cut through the aisles.

She remembered the job Frank had gotten her at Fernback's, cleaning the administrative offices. She had emptied trash cans, vacuumed the thin carpet. She'd found ways to cut corners and steal little things that she sold later. She didn't let Frank know this, and kept the little extra money for herself.

On Tuesdays and Thursdays some of the people on first shift would wait around in the parking lot to buy strawberries and beans from them. Frank spent part of his afternoons picking them and putting them into green cardboard cartons and half-bushel baskets to sell out of the trunk. He liked selling them, and could remember crawling around in his father's strawberry bed when he was a boy, eating until he made himself hivey and sick.

Those afternoons the sun shone off the windshields of the hundreds of cars lined up in the parking lot rows. *What else could any of us want out of life, than to be together?* the winking sun seemed to say. The strawberries tasted gritty and bitter to her. Those fields were most beautiful in the late dusk, the way the plants lay close to the red earth and made warm shadows as the sun went down.

One day while Frank had been in the fields, Eliza walked up the road to visit a good friend, the wife of another farming man. They sat in her kitchen with cups of coffee, the afternoon sun a thin strip through the curtains. Reba wore a pale green dress, tight around the waist, that came to just below her knees.

She did not work outside or have another job, and part of Eliza hated her for this.

They were talking about their husbands that day, Frank's endless work with the fruit and cleaning the factory, and the regimen of caring for the dozens of dairy cows and processing their milk. Eliza wanted to ask Reba about the exact moment they had fallen in love, if she still saw that in him when he came in for lunch. She was older than Eliza, and Eliza had always noticed the faint but beautiful lines around Reba's mouth and eyes.

A breeze blew through the open windows and threw the curtains open. Bright sun flickered across Reba's green dress and lit up her face and eyes. Eliza realized she would become this eventually, older, and for a second wanted to reach out and touch Reba, to put her mouth to hers, to fall onto the pale yellow linoleum of the kitchen floor with the pale green spread out across the floor. The moment pierced Eliza's heart, and she thought of it when the length of her days seemed something she would never escape.

Eliza walked deeper into the ringing slot machines, toward the card tables. She thought of that strange moment with Reba, and of the hours she and Frank had stolen at the factory, when instead of scrubbing toilets and emptying trash cans she had gripped his back and bitten the inside of his hand. So many times during those nights she had wanted to whisper, "Let's go away now," and the most desirous part of her had risen up and almost instantly she had become heartbroken. She lost a part of herself every time it happened. As time passed she wondered if anything would be left of her once it was over.

Eliza watched the dice fly across the craps tables and ran her hands down her hips. She had expected the casinos to be more glamorous, for the evidence of money to be everywhere. She didn't really see it, not in the cheap clothes or gaudy jewelry or the way people chased after the free drinks.

She stepped up to the edge of a table that still had room for players, and waited to be moved. She had heard that was the way some people gambled, that they would wait until the energy around them felt right, as if clairvoyance could be channeled in that way. Eliza didn't really believe in luck, but she did believe in being able to summon things. *How often does love last an entire lifetime?*

She stood between a young couple and a middle-aged man who reeked of booze. The young woman clung to the man's arm and whispered in his ear. He smiled and looked as if she had told him the winning numbers that would be rolled. They were dressed in blue jeans and cowboy boots.

The boy (she heard his name as Davis) had dark sideburns and wavy hair. The girl was pretty in a way that Eliza immediately envied. The kind of beauty that, like the saltwater in the air, would dry up all the spit in your mouth and fill you full of longing. She stood there until she was tired enough to want to go back to the hotel, her feet aching, and nothing touched her. She found Frank where she had left him at the nickel slots, his bucket of change almost gone.

That night they went to the ocean. Frank's heart beat harder as they walked down the beach. Eliza had never seen the ocean, either. Had never even learned to swim. The roar of the water was dull, but it caused the lights behind them to fall away for Frank. He pulled off his shoes and stood in the cold surf.

Eliza could not see where the black met the black. The chill started in her fingertips and went up her spine. *How do we get out of this? There is no way to get out of this.* The ocean was the biggest, darkest thing she had ever seen. There was no way to argue with it. There was nothing to do but face it.

"Let's come back in the morning," she said and pulled at his arm.

"Can you believe I've wanted to see this my whole life? Wanted to see it my whole life and it's so big it looks like it covers up half of the world?"

People walked near them. Ships blinked white and yellow in the distance. They marked the horizon, sailing towards a line they could never reach. Frank threw a handful of his nickels at the water.

"My whole life I wanted to see this, and now here it is!"

They turned and walked back toward where they would sleep. Away from the boardwalk they saw an old woman begging on the street. Her skin was white, but so mottled with dirt that it looked as if it had gotten wet in the rain and then dried on her in little rivulets. She walked slowly towards them, her ankles swollen with fluid. They looked away from her, trying not to let any change come across their faces. Frank saw the small graveyard of beer and Coke bottles underneath a tree as they walked past. There was no trash near the casinos.

Eliza watched two men across the street in front of a liquor store and wondered where people were buried in the city, especially in a place like Atlantic City, where most things already seemed a little dead. In eastern Kentucky they had a family plot up on a hill. Her father had taken her there and told her stories about the different stones. The cemetery was surrounded by bushes and blackberry vines on one side and an empty expanse of sky and blue mountain on the other. Eliza felt sad that she would not be buried there.

Their motel was a faded, peeling aqua. Across the street was a thrift store that did not open, and the faces of the mannequins in the windows had begun to crack and fall away. Eliza peered in one morning and saw the floor was a thicket of dust with the faint imprints of footsteps. There was a loud bar above the store. They could have gone to another place, but they did not.

Every day they noticed children waiting in the lobbies of the casinos. They looked bored sitting on the thick carpet. Somewhere within, their parents had forgotten about them. Eliza shook her head as she walked by, and thought of a better life for her own children.

Eliza felt a secret power after she and Frank separated. He hadn't liked the card tables when she took him to play, hadn't liked the closeness of other people or needing to depend on them. He played the machines with the same doggedness she'd always known him to work with.

Eliza became a beautiful woman again at the craps table. She watched the fast arc of the dice and felt as if she was waiting for something to happen that she could not make happen herself. She stood elbow to elbow with young men and women and old men with oiled gray hair. It was Thursday night, when the golden cacophony she had heard the first day invaded her again and she started winning. She saw the push and pull of the stacks of chips and could not remember why life had always seemed so hard. People wanted to stand next to her, and they looked at her as she had not been looked at since she was a teenager, and the waitresses brought drinks for everyone at the table. The pale green of her old friend's late summer dress came back to her, and all the days and nights in the long strawberry rows and corridors when her conscious mind, miraculously, did not have to think about what she was doing. Those things had always been the best she could hope for.

She drank until she was drunk and played until she started losing. A young man offered to help her find Frank. Her skirt clung to her hips. Frank was doe eyed when she found him. "Did you win anything?" he asked.

Their last night in Atlantic City, Frank mailed a cashier's check made out in the amount of all their winnings to their oldest daughter. She worked as a waitress in southeastern Ohio. The next morning they walked down to the beach in the early morning light, and the boardwalk had been mostly empty, just the gray early morning ghosts who hadn't yet gone to bed. The air on the beach was warm, not quite hot. There was still a hint of the night ocean chill in it.

Eliza had taken their original Atlantic City clothes to the cleaner the day before. They wore them as they walked on the beach, shoes in hand. The sand rolled under her black nylons. Frank carried one heavy bag, and his tired feet marveled at how good the sand felt. They had left the rest of their bags beside a trashcan on Tennessee Street. This included a handful of chips Eliza had not wanted to cash in. She had put them into the little compartment she had sewed into her bag.

They walked into the surf, mindful of the thin white scrim the ocean had etched onto the wet sand. The sand washed inside Eliza's stockings and she let it come up to her ankles. When they drew close to the pier they saw the pilings black with water and the clusters of white barnacles that grew on them.

"Maybe we should go up there?" she asked, and pointed up to the pier.

Frank nodded, but what his heart really wanted was to take her down onto the wet sand, the way he would have in the offices late at night. That desire opened up in him like the pale, thin slice of a quarter moon and he followed her up the beach. As he watched she dropped her shoes on the beach. He kicked sand over them as he walked past.

The concessions on the pier were all still closed. They walked beneath the place they had watched the motorcycle go over on a tightrope. Frank knelt and put on his black dress shoes. Eliza continued to walk on ahead of him. When they reached the end of the pier, she leaned over the rail and looked into the gray water. "It looks like a storm happened here," she said.

She turned, and with her back to the rail, began to take off her wet stockings. Frank saw how age had begun to curdle her once creamy skin. She looked completely naked without them.

Frank hoisted himself up onto the railing and sat with his legs dangling over the water. He breathed in the smell of the saltwater, so much different from the coal mountain air he was used to. He turned and helped Eliza up onto the railing beside him. He turned and put his hand high up on her leg, where the skin was warm and soft but infirm. He took a rope from the black bag beside him and tied it to her ankles. There was one cinder block inside the bag.

"If I swing this down would you be able to hold it up?" he asked.

Eliza shook her head.

"How do I know you'll come in after me?" she asked.

He looked at the gray line where the ocean met the sky. "I have to. There's nowhere else I want to go." He still had his hand on her thigh, and it felt like ice water when he withdrew it slowly, so that the trail of cold reached all the way down to her ankle.

"It's a wonder most people don't realize when they should die."

Eliza thought of the nights they had driven home together dog tired and soaked with sweat, and the whole time she had thought that was the beginning, and not the end.

He wound his foot into the tangle of rope and pushed the bag over the edge. He threw his hands above his head, and the rope jerked taut around their legs. They went down into the water, hands up and mouths open, as if they were riding one of the still-dormant roller coasters on the pier in the nighttime.

MANSION ON THE HILL

When I was a kid, our father took me and my sister Michelle to graveyards and our mother took us to look at the big new houses on the west side of town. Our father had stories to go along with the graveyards. I remember looking at the lichen that bloomed over the name etched on a headstone and squeezing my sister's hand while he talked about the person buried there. Our mother drove us over the black paved roads to look at the big houses and didn't say a word. Sometimes she drove up to a secret high place and we could see all of the burning lights of the houses spread out at once. In the summer, she rolled down the windows and the sound of night insects poured in. In the winter we listened to the silence of the frost.

The summer I was twelve years old Michelle and me started sneaking out of the house every weekend.

We told our parents we were spending the night with our girlfriend Julia who lived a few blocks away. I don't think they ever knew that most of our friends were boys. Sometimes we did actually stay with her, but most of the time we got on our bikes and met some of our other friends on the edge of the neighborhood. Michelle was just a year younger than me, and she kept up pretty well. She had a little red bike and I'd tied plastic onto the handlebars for her, so that when she rode fast it flapped in the wind and blew against her arms.

There was a dozen or so kids we rode out there with that summer, but only a handful always went. Benny was short and freckled, and his teeth looked like poorly cut LIK-EM-AID sticks. He was so skinny that his scarecrow body went with his Halloween smile. Nathaniel had long spiked hair the color of oily dishwater. He wore printed shirts that his mother got at a discount. They were two sided, so he could wear it on one side one day and on another the next. The shirts were so thin everyone caught on to his trick soon enough, and they gave him hell for it.

The kid I was closest to was a guy named Richie. He was good at drawing and he liked to show me pictures while we were in class. Sometimes they were things we'd seen on our bike trips. I told him that I wanted him to take up painting so he could start putting colors into his drawings.

John was kind of our leader. He was only a year older than me, but had thick muscles from helping his father do odd jobs on the weekends. When we were in the fourth grade, he'd asked if I wanted to see his dick while he pissed up against the brick wall of the school at recess. Some other girls had wanted to look and he shooed them away. "I just want Pamela to see this," he said. We walked to a corner by a gutter pipe and he pissed into the puddle that had gathered at the bottom of it. The pebbles and moss were clear under the rainwater and shimmered away when his piss hit the puddle. His dick was small and dirtyish beige and looked soft to the touch.

It was the first time I'd ever seen those parts, and it was startling but it was tender, too. He looked at me like he was giving me a gift, instead of waving around a weapon. I wonder if Mick, my oldest kid, has had anything like that happen to her. I wonder if I'll be able to tell when something does happen, if it'll be written on her face, or in the way she moves. Or if it'll be buried, so that no one will see it but her.

We all told our parents lies and met on a street corner that we changed every week. We biked to the outskirts of town, passing under streetlights into darkness and into the light again. The trees that lined the streets were huge and their shadows covered almost everything. We passed houses filled with the warm glow of lamplight and the chilly blue flickering of televisions.

The streetlights stopped at the town limits. We biked a little slower in the darkness. The smell of corn and dirt became that much thicker without the bright lights. The night sounds became louder. Even the dark seemed to have a smell and weight to it. Our voices carried far out there, ricocheting over the corn stalks before fading away. The place wasn't anywhere near as developed as it is now, and there was still a lot of farmland that hadn't been cleared away.

I fell in love with the motion of the bike rides, the sweep of the wind as we rode out into the darkness, the deep, heady smell of the corn. The ride was an expansive place between two points I felt like I couldn't escape. It came to be that I was always a little surprised when we finally got out to the west end neighborhoods. I just wanted to keep going, chasing some place that was past money and fancy brick and swimming pools. It's a place I still try to get to on the weekends, on the green county roads in my car.

The big houses were set far apart, but you could still tell they belonged together. The size of them said the same kind of people lived in all of them, just like the small, close-together houses we lived in said something about us. I'd never thought of the houses around me as small until we started going out there. The yards in our neighborhood were beaten flat, run over and well used. We knew almost all the kids who lived on the surrounding blocks. We saw each other every day at school and out in our yards. We saw into each other's rooms if the curtains were pulled back, and we overheard the sizzle of frying around dinnertime, the hateful fights between parents, and conversations on front porches that were supposed to be secret. We knew who was a drinker, who needed an abortion, who went away to jail.

I tried to imagine what people living out there did with all the space in their houses. Because of the Sunday trips with my father, I couldn't help but think of the tiny plots most people end up in. I wanted to ask my mother if she ever thought about this but was afraid to. I decided early on that I wanted to be scattered across the countryside when I died.

One night when we were out there, Michelle pulled me aside so the boys wouldn't hear her.

"What do you think the difference between us and them is?" she asked.

"What do you mean?" I asked back.

"I mean those kids that have big rooms like that and us."

I tried but wasn't able to answer. I thought about that look our mother got sometimes when we parked on the hill and looked at those houses spread out on the countryside. The question hung between me and Michelle until it became an awful feeling, a kind of twisted, hot desire. It was a dull shame that thudded at my temples and made a bitter taste at the back of my throat. For a little while, I imagined that living in a house like that would stop everything unpleasant, even death. I began to wonder if our father was preparing us for something by taking us to look at gravestones. I looked around at the boys in the moonlight, their narrowed eyes and fingers white on handlebar grips, and wondered if they'd had that feeling before.

In the summertime there was a party at one of those houses every weekend. We rode around until we found the house with the brightest lights and music and got as close as we could to it. We joked about sneaking into one of the parties and stealing liquor. All of us were too scared to do it, until finally one night John decided he would go in. We waited until very late on the edge of the lawn, our noses full of the smell of cut grass. Our bikes lay in a dull shining heap that weighed down the damp lawn in the moonlight. We watched John walk up the back deck steps and into the sliding glass door. We saw him move around through the well-lit windows. The people inside were so drunk that they paid him no mind. He came back with half a bottle of whiskey and half a bottle of vodka.

It was the first time I ever tasted whiskey. I was surprised at how it burned, but I loved it. We took sips of it carefully, as if it might turn on us suddenly, as if it had the power to make parts of us disappear. I wondered if one of the best things about growing up would be to be able to drink that stuff whenever I wanted to. I was twelve years old.

Michelle and I wanted to tell our mother about all the things we had seen when she drove us around to look at the houses. We wanted her to talk, to hear what she had to say about them. We wanted to know why she kept such a distance, why she parked up on a hill instead of driving right through the neighborhood.

One night when we were out there, I recognized a girl we went to school with through one of the brightly lit plate glass windows. She was getting ready for bed, and I watched each of her familiar movements with fascination. The boys elbowed each other, hoping she would take her shirt off. I became breathless. Here was someone I *knew*, someone I saw in the hallways, and she had no idea I was watching her.

"I'd love to make that rich bitch suck my dick," Benny said, grinning with his big teeth.

John laughed at him. "You dumb fuck. You'd be lucky if you could get her fucking dog to suck your dick."

When she turned off the light Michelle looked at me and I could tell she was glad the light was out. I let out my breath in a big huff, and we all moved across the damp grass to look into another house. The boys liked to watch people go to bed through open windows. We all liked to watch them, even if there were only silhouettes. It made my skin crawl, but like the whiskey, it made me wonder about being grown up and being able to touch naked bodies when I wanted, and being able to make what I wanted of my own body. The older I got, the more I appreciated what John had done that day by the school, that he had helped me get ready for a moment that would come barreling down at me, whether I was ready for it or not, soon enough.

I watched Cindy closely for the next few days at school, silently awed by her. I had so many questions that I wanted to ask her, but didn't know how. I wanted to know what her mom and dad did for a living. I wanted to know how big her bedroom was. I wanted to ask her why she undressed with the lights turned off. Curtains and shades were pulled over most of the bedroom windows. Were they afraid that someone was out there, waiting to steal anything from them, even their solitude? These must have been the unspoken things on our minds when we dared each other to go closer and closer to the sleeping houses, up under the wide pressure-treated decks, past the humming central air systems, up to the tiny, infinite checker board of screen that protected them from the rest of the world as they slept. Out there we had something on them, if only for a few hours. They didn't know who we were or what we were capable of.

I don't know how I would feel about my own kids doing similar things. I want them to have something that will give them strength in the hard days ahead, and I understand it will probably be something that

I will never know about. This is one of the heart-breaks of being a parent, that you can never know your children as complete people.

Sometimes when I take them to visit their aunt and uncle and first cousins I remember the creature I became on those bike rides. I look at them standing quiet in the big white foyer waiting for one of their cousins to talk to them. The power I found went with me everywhere, but it made me grow up faster. It was like sediment that dropped down through me, outlining every vertebra and rib, and turning them to stone. I hope they have some secret.

The last time Michelle and me went out to the west end we were with John, Benny, Richie, and a couple of other boys I didn't know very well. There had been a thunderstorm earlier that evening, just as the sun was going down. Ozone and electricity were heavy in the air. The remaining clouds were outlined purple and silver by the moon. The rest of the sky was a deep velvet midnight punctured by the clear light of the stars.

We had found shortcuts on the farm roads that cut through the fields to the neighborhoods. That night John stopped his bike at the top of a gentle slope. In the distance I could see the lights of the big houses above the corn stalks. We all stopped, John ahead of us, my sister and I in the middle, three other friends behind us.

John had been moody all day in school, and Richie finally told me that his mother had been fired the day before. She'd worked as a housekeeper in a big motel outside of town. John had come home from school the day before and she'd been sitting at the kitchen table, still in her uniform, smoking cigarettes.

He turned around to us, his bike still between his legs. He was shaking in the moonlight and looked like he might cry. He wrapped his arms around himself and the muscles flickered. "I think we should burn down every goddamn place we can up there," he said. "I'm tired of crawling around here at night. I want this fucking place to be gone." The rest of us looked at him, the rich smell of wet corn and earth in our noses.

I felt Michelle get tense beside of me. "I don't think we should do that," she said. Everyone else was silent for a minute. John brought his arms down to his sides. He sat low on his bike, so that the fork of his legs rested on the bar.

"You just don't fucking get it, do you? Sometimes you have to do something crazy to get people to think about you."

"We can't do that. If you gonna do that then I'm going home," Michelle said. She suddenly seemed about eight years old.

John looked at her like he might kill her. He got off his bike. He turned his flat, angry gaze towards me and I realized part of why he was looking at me was

42

because I was a girl. I thought of that day by the school wall, and it made me shudder.

"You gonna make your sister shut up, or am I gonna have to figure out a way?" he asked, not quite smiling.

I felt the way John was looking at us spread to the other boys. They snickered behind us. Benny grabbed my elbow and held me. I thought about his comment about Cindy sucking his cock. This is what our parents would be afraid of, I thought. Richie looked at me guiltily, but the guilt wasn't the only thing that was on his face. They had their own smell, and it came off them like the oily and stale, like the air in a room that has been closed up for years.

Something shifted between us, powerful and dark. It passed over us quickly and left the air charged, like the electric storm a few hours before. They knew I wasn't one of them anymore, if I ever really had been. They looked at us and seemed to move in closer. I was conscious for the first time of how my small nipples poked at my T-shirt. I understood that it wouldn't be safe to go out with all of them again. I also understood how important it was that my mother and father never find out that my sister and I were running out at night with a bunch of boys.

Seeing them like that must have scared Michelle to death. It scared me too, but the fear turned into something else, some kind of strength that I could draw on. It was the first time I ever really thought about what it meant to be a girl. It might have been my words that broke up the thunderclouds when I wrenched my arm free of Benny. "Fuck off, John. You're not going to do shit," I said. I stood glaring at them for a few moments and it was suddenly over. The spell broken, we started pedaling on our bikes again. I was wet with sweat and scared. I knew that if anything had happened to my sister and me, the neighborhood would have agreed in hushed tones that we deserved it for running around with them.

I had been all set to tell her why it wasn't a good idea to go on bike rides with them anymore, but she brought it up first. "I'm not going to sneak around out there anymore," she said. "The next time I go there I'll be inside one of those houses."

Michelle was different after that trip. She started to hate everything we were surrounded with, like just living where we did would make us mean and no good. She hated the way the yards were small and full of things, the way younger kids were loud on the sidewalks, the way the cooking smells hung in the air in the evening. She hinted that our parents were lazy, that they had wasted their lives. "I don't understand why our parents do what they do. I don't understand why they didn't choose something different, something better," she said.

I still don't really know anything about our parents' lives, just as they don't know much about their kids' lives. I don't know what choices they had, or what they thought was possible for them. How can you erase whole generations of ideas? My sister didn't bother trying to erase where she'd come from. She made an entirely new past and placed it right over the old, so that even when it showed through you couldn't tell what it was, like a reflection in a soaped over window.

Our parents miss her. She never comes to visit them. I know they feel like some part of them has been cut out, and in a way it has. To keep from feeling outside of something, my sister has put up a wall to keep her old self out.

There is talk that the steel mill our father worked at will be moving out of town in the next couple of years. I'm thankful that he has already retired. I wouldn't be able to stand watching him trying to find a new job, an old man trying to convince employers that his old skills are worth something. I am not so scared for myself. There is something hard in me, and I will be able to stand on it until I die.

I see John almost every day at work. He looks at me like he thinks I don't belong there, like there is something he doesn't like about my heavy boots and flannel shirts. We never really talked after that night in the corn. I wonder if he remembers the smell my sister and I must have given off, something half fear and half sex. I wonder if Michelle remembers it too, if she smells those things like crackling ozone whenever she doesn't return our parents' phone calls or when she tells her children to be careful around mine.

I drive my mother to look at those houses sometimes now. There are many new ones. I want to tell her about the cornfields, about the things we used to do as children, but I do not. I am careful not to drive by my sister's house. She is still silent on these rides, but sometimes she cries. I cannot tell if she is crying because she misses my sister or because she misses her entire life. I ask her if my father still visits graveyards and she nods yes. Her hair is long, almost completely gray. It has the lovely coarseness of a horse's mane.

JOHNNY 99

Ralph drove one of the cars he used to build. After the auto plant closed down, he thought about shooting out its tires every time he looked at it. He thought about taking it apart and selling the pieces for scrap metal or burying them in the yard. One night he got so drunk he thought about eating the goddamn thing and getting rid of it that way.

The factory still stood on a hill on the west side of town. The parking lot still fanned out from the building, but it was always empty. Ralph wondered if the buildings were empty on the inside too, if all the machinery and parts had been gutted out of there and shipped to some new place overseas, or if it was cheaper to let them slowly go to rust and darkness and scavengers. It didn't seem like anything new would fill the building anytime soon.

His mother cried when she heard the plant was moving. Ralph stood stock still, the sleeves of his blue shirt rolled up. The flicker of a muscle in his jaw was his only movement before he walked out into the bright blue of the afternoon and drove directly to the bar he went to sometimes on the weekends.

The company gave a month's notice, but Ralph quit the same day they told them. The next morning he left to find a job when his wife went to work. He drove his car slowly up the main avenue. He couldn't remember the last time he had been out on a weekday. He drove along parallel streets for miles in both directions, talking to people and filling out applications. He stopped at a drive-in hamburger stand for lunch and leaned against the trunk of his car while he ate. A boy and a girl, not quite teenagers, walked across the weed-plagued parking lot with their arms hooked over big skateboards. They were tan and dirty and their ankles were bare. Ralph watched them until they were out of sight and then got back in the car.

The sky above the pavement was pale blue. It was late August and the heat of summer was still in the air, but he could feel that it was tempered with something thinner and cooler. He wondered if the kids were cutting school already or if it was too early for school to start. He drove around for the rest of the day, dropping off applications and asking questions, feeling the difference between knowing where he was going each day and suddenly having no idea what would happen next. Wherever he looked reminded him of it, from the rough listless teenagers with skateboards to the thin lines of wire the streetlights were strung from.

A week later, he drove back around to the places where he had left applications and talked to people. "That's rough, the plant leaving like that," was what most people said. No one seemed to remember his name or face. Some of them wanted to talk politics, to bad mouth the people that would be getting their old jobs sooner or later. "They're all foreigners, that'll be putting together those cars. I don't buy it unless I know it was made here by guys like you," one woman said and pointed towards his chest.

Ralph nodded at this but it wasn't really a reply to her. He just wanted her to shut up. He didn't feel like he had in him to think about the rest of the world, or hate the people in places he would never see. He did not have room for anyone else's problems or fears. His part of the earth was hard enough just the way it was.

As he looked for a job, he realized he was on the other side of a line he had never known existed. No place, not the dark, oil-smelling garages or the grease-filled restaurants, offered him any work. Everyone's faces at the last few places he went back to, whether they were behind a counter or dressed in a mechanic's uniform, drew up tight and cold. In a week he had become someone who was somehow beneath anyone who drew a paycheck, an enemy because he was standing in line, waiting to take anything a working man wouldn't stand for. This is what their faces said about him, but it was not how he felt.

One night at dinner he almost told his girlfriend about the car shooting fantasy.

"How'd it go today?" she asked as they ate fried potatoes and corn. The thick bone of a pork chop lay brown and bare on his plate.

"Not much out there," he said. They don't even want to look at me, he wanted to add. The sun had disappeared but the light from beyond the horizon made the sky a clear bright dark blue. A tree outside the kitchen window had turned completely black.

"I think I'll go for a drive after dinner," he said.

"You want any company?"

"No, I'll be back soon," he said and pushed himself away from the table.

Ralph looked at the car parked in the short driveway as he stood on the lawn. The whole neighborhood was heavy with the smells of dinner frying. The wide chrome grille of the old Ford was like a great crooked smile in the faded light. He saw the separate parts of the car, spread out and moving down an assembly line. He saw the hundreds of hands that had touched those parts. The thud of the door when he slammed it cut off the night sounds. He had no idea where he was going.

He turned on the radio, the line of the dial pale against the luminescent green of the dashboard lights. The radio was the only thing in the car that he really wanted to keep, but even it had started to betray him. The songs on the rock station began to take on new meanings and sometimes he pulled the car into mostly empty parking lots and held his face in his hands. They were big and rough and would grow softer as the weeks went by.

He drove away from town, towards the darkness of the outlying county. He thought about Sheila at home washing the dishes, the way her hair would look through the kitchen window in the light, the way she stooped her shoulders over the sink. She had a job working as a seamstress. He had no idea how long it would last. She had told him she sewed blue jeans, and had run her hand up his thigh to show him the long seam she sewed on hundreds of pairs of pants. The jeans were just like the cars, everybody doing one thing and then passing it along.

The darkness outside of town swelled; the sun was long gone. The Rolling Stones came on the radio and Ralph remembered a drive he had taken years before with his closest friend. They hadn't been out of high school long and winter had just started. It was dark and cold and the fields were frosted over. The same song came on the radio and he had sat still listening to it, his friend singing along beside him. He had felt like he understood every word of it, and for a moment he saw his entire life as they drove, clear and crystalline as the frost outside. Even in the cold he had felt something in him as hot as a meteor shower. The feeling stayed with him for days and slowly began to fade away. Hearing the song again, he couldn't really recall the feeling or when he had forgotten it. It was another cut out shape in the darkness, the edges of it hinting at brightness.

He rolled down the window and let the wind blow across his face. He sang the lyrics loudly and felt like he almost remembered the feeling again and then it was gone. He thought about the daylight hours in town and suddenly they did not make sense. He thought about the inside of the auto plant, still moving and assembling each day, and the hundreds of bodies that were not quite out of work. He pounded the steering wheel and felt angry with himself for not possessing a strength that he couldn't even name.

When he walked into the house Sheila was getting ready for bed. He didn't realize he'd been gone so long. She took one look at his face and didn't ask him where he had driven. She looked tired herself. The bedroom light seemed cloying and oppressive, and he snapped it off before he pulled off his clothes and got into bed.

As the days went by, Ralph began to see parts of the town he'd never noticed. The vacant lots of closed-down grocery stores and auto parts places had a life of their own. People passed through them at different times and congregated before moving on. The walls and pavement were covered with graffiti. He saw the secret, wide open places teenagers escaped to. He didn't know how to share these things with anyone.

He started to duck into small bars in the middle of the day; each had its own dark, cavernous personality. The dim spaces reminded him of the repetition of a working day, and they were a comfort. He remembered the certainty of knowing what each day would look like before it began and thought of the thin balance of the possibility of everything and nothing. Ace's, the bar so many of his friends from the Ford plant went to, became fuller on weekday nights. It was fuller all the time, even in the middle of the afternoon. Sometimes he stopped in and he and his old co-workers—the other guys who had quit—bought each other drinks in cautious ways. They had a jump on the others but they were still felt like they were getting nowhere.

He wondered if he should let up looking for work when he began having vivid dreams of cutting the car into small pieces with a blowtorch and swallowing them. Sometimes he woke up with a terrible pain in his stomach and would lie awake while Sheila breathed quietly beside him.

He didn't tell her about his night pains and awful dreams and he didn't tell her that he could keep on looking for work everyday and not have any luck because there was none to be had. Most of the people who had jobs looked thin and desperate, like they might lose them any time. It was a thinness behind the eyes that he saw, a leanness that came not from having too little to eat, but from having too little of everything.

The first day he didn't look for anything he parked to save gas. He walked around a neighborhood and tried to think of ways to bring in money. A low, desperate thought like the whine of a faraway insect began at the back of his head. He couldn't push it away as he walked. He knew to keep the house he could either start gambling or start stealing. And he knew which one seemed like the surer bet.

He walked into Ace's and sat heavily on a stool. His shoulders drooped and the bartender took pity on him by giving him a free drink. The bars were one of the only places still making good money. Instead of starting out with a beer he had Tanqueray and tonic. The smell of it was high and evil and reminded him of the juniper trees that had grown in his grandmother's yard.

By the time seven o'clock rolled around, he was encased in drunkenness. He watched the streets grow dark outside and felt absolutely comforted by the darkness and the loud voices around him growing louder. His friend Daniel came in and sat by him. They had come to know each other on the rivet line, connecting the bare skeletons of what would become Ford cars and trucks. They were the beginning, three days from where the assembly line opened up to the sky and the vehicles emerged complete, with no sign that hundreds of hands had gone into making them.

They often spent their lunch breaks together, drinking quick beers from a cooler Daniel kept in the cab of his truck. They knew each other well, and Daniel thought Ralph had become very different after he'd stopped working, like when he moved he was expecting something inside of him to break. After Ralph was arrested Daniel would think that the way he had moved made perfect sense.

Daniel asked the bartender for bourbon and they toasted.

"So how long do you have left?" Ralph asked.

"Two more days and then we're out of there."

"You know there ain't nothing out here to have, right? I've been looking for almost a month, every-day, and there ain't nothing."

"Don't tell me that shit. I didn't come here to hear that."

"Well, look around," Ralph said. "Seems like the only thing in demand around here is bartenders."

"Ralph, I came here to get drunk. Are you going to help me or not?"

Ralph tipped back his drink and tried to smile. "You're the working man. You want to get me a drink, then I'll help you out," he said.

Daniel ordered him another gin and tonic. More guys they knew flooded in. They ordered beers and clapped each other on the back. Most of them just looked tired, like if they worked harder, their jobs would not disappear. The pool tables in the back clacked with a maddening regularity. The faces above them were drawn and serious under the fluorescent lamps.

Ralph and Daniel sat down at a table with Jeff, a big man who was still working at the plant. He was wearing blue jeans and a heavy flannel shirt. The jukebox thumped. A smile spread across Ralph's face, but it was bitter. "There's a big difference between working and not working," he finally said.

"I guess you know better than us," Jeff said. "We're all still there. Why the hell did you leave so soon, anyway?"

"Yeah," Daniel said, joking with him. "You got some money stashed away or something?"

"I don't have a damn thing stashed. I've been all over this town while you've been working every day. There ain't nothing here. There's no place for you to go, and no one gives a fuck about it, not even a lot of the people you're working with."

"You think a bunch of people are going to move away from here?"

"They're going to have to, unless they want to see everything they own spread out on their front lawn."

"Shit," Daniel said. "That's a job I wouldn't want to have. The man who comes around like that."

"At least you wouldn't feel too bad if you were out of a job," Jeff said. "What do you think's worse," he asked, "losing everything or being the one to make a person let go?"

The song ended. Daniel laughed but he didn't mean it. "I guess some things are worse than dying," he said.

Ralph laughed at that. "You know, a month ago, I wouldn't have believed that. But I think I'm starting to understand now."

They all got shitfaced that night and it was like a pure, falling joy.

In the next few months many families moved away. The streets became quieter. Lots of people who had worked at the plant noticed because they had time to notice. Daniel was lucky enough to get a part-time job bartending at night. Some people who stayed found jobs and others lost everything because they didn't know where to go. Families did end up with everything they had out on the sidewalk, beds and dressers out of place next to the grass, and Ralph wondered who in the hell had the heart to do that to them. He remembered the conversation he had with Daniel and Jeff, about how some things are worse than death.

Both men followed the story in the papers as more and more people left town. After Ralph was thrown in jail, Daniel wondered if he was still able to follow the papers from his cell. It was the biggest news in Mahwah for a while. He became Ralph even to the folks who had known him well, named after the sentence the judge had given him. It was almost like the papers were relieved they had something else to talk about, like it was good there was something worse going on than the bigger picture, like all the badness going around could be put in one man and sent away.

Daniel felt like he still saw Ralph because of all the boys that came into the bar that reminded him of him. They came in and ordered a drink their faces were different from the other people in the room, chin tilted just a little towards the ceiling. Nobody would call it being stuck-up unless they were afraid of it.

Daniel didn't believe alcohol was always desperation, even when he saw people do desperate things because of it. He knew that more often than not there was something underneath it. The same night Ralph shot that night clerk, the bartender where he and Ralph were drinking said he thought things would start looking up. Daniel snorted when he said that. It had gotten cold, and the town had taken on the rotten gray that hangs on from November until the end of February.

For better or for worse, it was one of those nights when the bartender started pouring drinks for free and just didn't stop because he was in a good mood. Daniel had nights like that himself bartending, when he felt like the work he was doing was similar to preaching, and he was happy and proud to share a little joy.

Daniel had joked back at the bartender that night.

"When things start looking up in here means the rest of the world has gone to shit," he'd said. They turned from the bar and grabbed one of the tables facing the street. Daniel noticed Ralph's dark hair was getting longer. There was a convenience store right across the street, and it was busy all night with teenagers cruising and people buying gas and beer. Once when there was no one he knew in the bar, Daniel had watched the comings and goings of the parking lot all night long.

When they sat down, Ralph started in. "I've been thinking a lot lately about what makes life worth living," he said. "I don't think I ever really thought about it before I got laid off. One of things I've noticed, going around here looking for a job and hanging out in bars, is that no one seems all that happy. The people working seem miserable at it, and the people not working seem miserable because they're scared."

Daniel looked at him flatly, stunned that he'd never noticed it before. It seemed so obvious to him that there was no reason to even say it out loud. It was like the sameness of a working day, something you had to train yourself not to notice or it'd drive you crazy.

"What I mean," Ralph said, "is why keep on at something that isn't doing you any good? Why not change it up, try something different? I never even really knew that I had choices until I found out the company was leaving. I might have known it sometime when I was really young, but I forgot."

"You really think you just forgot?" Daniel asked.

Ralph thought back to listening to "Paint it Black" on the radio, how the memory that feeling just after high school had come back and then gone again. It was that last part, the feeling of losing something not once, but over and over again, that made him feel so terrible.

He sighed. "I did forget. Or maybe I just never really knew in the first place. If you're the only one who knows something, then it's easy to forget it."

They sat in silence for a minute. Daniel had a pitcher of beer in front of him. The parking lot across the street filled up and emptied out.

"That plant leaving was a real kick in the teeth," Daniel said, "but we've got to figure out a way to keep on going."

"I've already decided," Ralph said, "that the way I keep on with things won't be anything like how I've been living." He looked at Daniel and swallowed part of his drink. "I feel like I've figured out a lot of things I didn't know before."

They talked on into the night. Daniel finished his pitcher and started in on another. He said goodbye to Ralph for the last time without really thinking about it.

Daniel would wonder again and again what happened to Ralph after he left the bar that night. When he pictured it, it was like a movie, with the ignition being switched on and the headlights coming up and splashing all over the dim streets. He imagined the car moving unsteadily, but he couldn't see where it went.

Ralph drove home when he left the bar. The streets were mostly empty. He drove slow and was careful to stop at all the lights. In his head he dared an officer to stop him. The deep, false joy that drinking had brought him over the preceding weeks was gone. He felt irritation and unease instead. It lived under his skin, in his muscles. He started to see a way out of his predicament. It was a dark way, but it still had some kind of light at the end of it.

When he got home, Sheila took a look at him and seemed to know what he was gonna do. "Do you need me to drive you?" she asked. Her lips were tight, her mouth stony, but it was different from the daily drawn look that had taken over her features. This one seemed powerful. It said I'm not defeated; I'm just getting started.

Ralph went to their bedroom and took his pistol from the bedside table. It was the same gun he pictured having in his hands when he thought about slowly shooting row after row of Fords, the heavy glass shattering into pellets, the metal opening and smoking. She seemed about to stop him when he stepped out the kitchen door. She stood in the doorway until he was almost on her and then she stepped out of the way. Her eyes were wide and dark. The night air was cold.

She watched him get in the car and back out of the short driveway. He had become strangely sober by then; a deep calm widened his chest. He switched the radio off and drove to a popular convenience store. He parked and stared at himself in the mirror. His face looked harder. He kept trying to look away from it but could not.

He opened the car door and walked across the oil-stained parking lot of the gas station. It was almost empty. He opened the door and dimly heard the little bell jingling. He started by asking the clerk a question and then he raised the gun up and pointed it at her chest. When Daniel thought about it, he always tried to imagine what Ralph said. Most of the time he couldn't hear anything, just see his lips moving through the glass. But sometimes he got whole sentences: "I don't want to hurt you, just give me what money you've got in there." Sometimes he would go on to tell her about Sheila, sometimes he would just talk about how lucky she was to have a job at all.

The clerk was a tough one and she saw how the desperation in Ralph's face was moving him from young to old. She wanted to tell him that life would get a lot harder, that he'd better learn to bear up under it. "No one deserves to get it easy," she'd whispered as she reached for something underneath the counter. Ralph squeezed the trigger and she flew back against the wall.

Someone came into the store and then backed out again. She ran until she got to a payphone up the block and started dialing the cops. Ralph stood still out in the parking lot and stared up at the bright streetlights. It had started to rain. The dull shine of his dark boots was the same color as the oil stains on the pavement. He ran hard but without any real conviction when he heard the sirens and the noise filled up his ears.

The pavement was slick and black with rain. Traffic lights and taillights streaked up the black asphalt. When Ralph's face hit the pavement, it got caught in the red glow. He was yelling something at the cops over and over again, over all the talk and sirens. The cops put the cuffs on him rough and pushed him into the back of the patrol car. It didn't take long for the crowd that had gathered to thin out.

Ralph tried to get everything he could out of his lawyers and Sheila about the woman he'd shot. She was an older woman, with a couple of kids and a new grandbaby. The mother of it was very young. The woman he'd killed had worked at the gas station for many years. He cried when he asked Sheila about it, the hardness in his face melting away to defeat. He saw himself high over the chasm he'd tried to jump across, not yet plummeting down, just hanging there, waiting for whatever would come next. There were a few people calling out for the death penalty, but the DA didn't try to push it.

A few weeks after the trial, Daniel called Sheila to find out what had happened in court and they met up at Ace's. She didn't cry when she told him, but her eyes were dry and hard and bright, like everything in them had been polished out.

"I don't remember exactly what he said. I wish I had it recorded so I could just play it back for you. He stood up and swallowed and tried to tell the judge about the plant closing down, about how he'd lost his job and didn't know where it was going. He tried to tell the judge that he just wanted the money, that he tried to talk to the woman, that he didn't understand why she had wanted to shoot someone who was so much like her, especially over some money that wasn't hers anyway.

"And when he said that someone had stood up from that woman's family screaming, 'You ain't nothing like her! Nothing like her!' I thought they'd have to lead the guy out of there.

"And then he asked to be killed. Said it clear and flat like it was no big deal. He told that judge that if he really understood the difference between justice and vengeance, then he would go ahead and have him killed, because the world would be better off with him dead than in jail."

"But the judge gave him life anyway, didn't he?" Daniel asked, even though he already knew the answer. He got a picture of his old friend sitting in the electric chair and it made him shudder. The thought of him shuffling around prison as an old man made him shudder even more. He found out from Sheila that his visiting days were Tuesday and Saturday, but never went to see him.

HIGHWAY PATROLMAN

There's a place out by the Nolichucky River I used to go to before I took the deputy job. In the summer you can smell the green coming off the river and the coming cold blowing down from the woods on Iron Mountain. There's still music down there on the weekends, country and bluegrass and every once in a while rock 'n' roll. I used to go and dance all the time after my brother Frank took me for the first time. I've even puked a time or two in the gravel parking lot, the rocks and dirt tearing through my pants and leaving red marks on my knees. The guy that owns it lives above it, so on warm nights he'd leave the deck open so people too drunk to drive home could sleep it off. I've stayed out there a time or two myself, and waking up hung over to the bright light of the sun feels like waking up in hell.

Joel Monahans has been running Chucky's for as long as I can remember. He's getting to be an old man now, and I think he's seen more teenagers lose their virginity on his back porch and in his parking lot than some of the more well-known whores in town. Joel and his place are one of the most important things in this town, whether the church-going establishment wants to admit it or not.

Chucky's is a friendly place if you know how to act. Most of the boys (a few women, but mostly boys) that come down there come straight out of the mountains. From Flag Pond and Limestone Cove and from even further back. There's fights there all the time, but I hardly ever have to go down there. They know that for the most part they're all in the same boat, and it ain't gonna do them any good to stab or shoot each other. Sometimes there's a fist-fight in the gravel and Joel breaks them up by threatening not to let them come back. It's a town with no other drinking holes, and they usually listen.

There's not much in the way of work around here. Most people would rather draw than work at the goddamn McDonald's and I don't blame them. The luckier ones work at a couple of factories—one makes camera film, the other car, truck, and tractor tires—and the not so lucky ones hire themselves out as farmhands or pull moss on the side. I did that one summer when I was growing up and it was horrible work, the moss wet and full of bugs, the undersides of it crumbling mud. Still, most people who go to school here end up dying here, and the people who move here usually end up staying. They're hard men, some of them desperate, and maybe because I was a little less desperate or a little more lucky, I got the job of keeping them in line.

Hard work and not enough money will make some people mean after a while. I get to see that real close-up sometimes, usually going up into some house where a man has beat his wife half to death. There's some people that just want to pick a fight, and the kind that don't understand why whatever made life enjoyable would dry up and die. There's the meanness that every man is born with, that comes to him even as a child. Some are good at fighting it and some let it come out, either all at once or slow and bitter. My brother Frank was like that, and nobody cared much when he left for Nashville straight out of school.

Frank wanted to be a country singer more than anything else and that was what made him different from the hoods he ran around with. His senior year he played in the high school talent show, just him and an acoustic guitar, and I sat there wiping my eyes the whole time. His voice when he sang was bigger than the one I was used to. He played a Guy Clark song and one of his own, and the audience clapped up a storm when he was done. People were afraid of him, and that made him special.

But mixed in with that hope for him to be something great was the hatred of the other things I knew he was capable of. It was ugly, but it was there, like the dozens of clumsy initials scratched into the wooden auditorium seat in front of me. Our school was so old that some of those people were probably dead by the time I was a sophomore. Thinking about those two sides of him made me feel like I was being ripped apart, and I wondered how he could stand to live inside himself. His voice had a low twanging gravel that was just like the woods on the Nolichucky where we'd both spent so much time running around. I remember it now and wonder if a body can do time for the crimes of someone else, for that person you might have been ten or twelve or even fifty years ago.

I never really wanted to be a cop. I planned to keep the land my father had kept, just like he'd kept it from my grandfather. It wasn't what I really wanted, but it was the best thing I could think of. Me and my wife Maria lived in the same big farmhouse me and Frank grew up in. It sat in the middle of the big fields our family had planted and hoed and harvested, the same fields me and Frank had run around in, daring each other to stare into the darkest part of the woods as the dusk came in through the rows of corn beans and tobacco.

I took over the farm after my father died. My mother was gone right after him. I was just twenty years old, and Frank had run off to Nashville three years before. I wasn't as good with the land as our daddy had been, and I wasn't sure that I ever really wanted to be. He was content to work until he was limp as a rag at the end of the day and then get up the next day and do it all over again. He was content to work that hard and never have anything. When he died he was fifty-five; he had arms that were big and stringy with muscle. The kind of arms you'd be afraid of, but covered in gray hair.

I never heard much from Frank the years he was gone. As the bills piled up, I started to imagine that he'd come along to bail us out. The longer he was gone, the surer I was he must've made it. I kept waiting for him to call or to hear him on the radio, for him to tell me he had the money that would keep our family's land from getting whittled away each year. Frank did come back, but not until after I'd lost the whole damn thing. The rooms we'd grown up in, the yard, the fields, and the woods, none of it was ours to go to anymore.

After that Maria and I started renting a little house in town and I took the deputy job. The guys I'd always run with started talking to me less. They acted like I would start coming down on them for the little things they always did. I stopped going to

Chucky's a little at a time, and now I don't go down on the river unless I've got a call.

I think Maria might have been with Frank if he hadn't gone away. She was older than both of us, and I'd met her one night down at Chucky's when I was still in high school. The only half-Mexican in the whole goddamn county, but she didn't get much shit for it because she was so beautiful. She got shit in a different way instead. Me and Frank had just come down off of Iron Mountain a few weeks before that, and I was scared every time he left the house alone. That night I asked him if I could go to Chucky's with him, if he thought they would let me in.

Frank had laughed at me. "Shit, that place'll let anybody in. Anytime you want to go, little brother, let me know."

We got into his van. He'd cleaned it out, but I thought I could still see stains on the black runners in the back, but they must have been my imagination. He caught me looking and grinned. "Gonna get that shit carpeted soon. Know what I mean little brother?"

I nodded and watched the dark road pass around us. We pulled into the gravel parking lot and I became terrified that Frank was going to leave me. I didn't really even know how to drink then.

"You know a lot of these people?" I asked him.

"You know I do," he said.

I slid down from the high seat of the van and my boots hit the gravel. I don't think I'll ever forget that sound. It was the same as hearing a houseful of doors slamming shut behind you, one after the other. That whole summer was like a thousand slamming doors for me. That's what growing older has always felt like to me; you just go till you get to the end.

I followed Frank up the wooden steps and through the front door. It was hot and loud inside, and I recognized a lot of people from school. The rest were older. Road hookers and bikers and farmers and bands all mixed in together. Sometimes Frank played shows down there, but I never saw him.

He bought me a whiskey and then left me alone. I leaned up against a wall and started talking to some friends of mine from school. Over their shoulders, I watched Frank in action. For a little while the love I had for him surpassed anything else, and I was proud of how people seemed to hang off him and buy him drinks. They all thought he was going to be a big star, but it was more than that, too. Like he had something they wanted, and might be able to get by being near to him.

Later on, when I was good and drunk, Frank came over and told me he had someone he wanted me to meet. We went out on the back deck and there sat Maria Cigarroa at a table by herself, surrounded by empty pitchers and glasses.

"This here's my little brother Travis," Frank said, his arm around my neck and one hand on her shoulder.

"I seen you around," she said, and I blushed.

"Yeah. Good to meet you," I said. The straps of her white flowered dress had fallen off her shoulders. Me and Frank sat down at the table.

We talked on and on. And drank more and more. She looked at me and Frank the same way, and that seemed strange to me. That old Bobbie Gentry song, "Fancy," came on the jukebox and she got up and did a dance for us. Her lips fit with that white woman's heavy, Southern voice. And I started to fall in love with her body, the way a young person who's never really seen a body before will. They way someone who hasn't understood that they might be able to touch someone else's body will. I'm still not sure exactly what it means to fall in love, but part of it must have happened to me that night.

When she sat down sweating from the dance and the heat, Frank slid over to her and kissed her on the mouth. I watched him trace down to her neck and the hollow of her shoulder with his finger, like he'd done it before. I got up to leave, to go hang out with those buddies of mine who weren't getting laid either.

When I pushed my chair back, Maria touched my hand. "Where you goin, Travis?" she asked. And before I could answer she'd leaned across the table and put her lips on mine.

My hands reached up like I was drowning and grabbed her soft brown shoulders. I kissed her back and forgot Frank watching us.

"Y'all want to come out the van?" I heard him say. And in that drunk way I'd get used to in the coming years, we stumbled out to the van like angels had us by our shirt collars and tumbled into the back.

I knew well enough what my brother's cock looked like, but I'd never seen anything like Maria before. She was so fucking beautiful. And the only thing I could think while I watched him fuck her was, "You better be glad you so fucking beautiful, cause these animals would tear you apart if you weren't."

When Frank crawled back from Nashville fourteen years after he'd left, both our parents were dead from cancer and the farm was already gone. I'd been a deputy for three years. He stayed with me and Maria the first few months, in that little apartment in the middle of town, sleeping on the couch. He'd come home late sometimes and just cuss. "These country fucks," he'd say. "How the fuck you stand em Travis? You supposed to protect these people and they ain't even worth the air wasted on em to breathe."

He said this while laying on the couch, one of our mother's old quilts wrapped up around him. Frank never wanted to talk about what had happened to him in Nashville. Sometimes I tormented him with it when he was too drunk to move, too drunk to do anything but shake and nod and drool.

"What happened to you, country star?" I said. "Where's the devil that was supposed to have your back? Did you lose him on your way over the mountains?"

Those nights I should have been in bed to be able to go to work in the morning, Maria was asleep, and I sat at his bedside, watching him snore, with my gun slid out of its holster, the metal nosed right up against his numb jaw. I wanted to kill him for the thing he'd done to me, but I couldn't. Night after night I left the safety on and clicked the trigger home, but it was dry.

Some people loved Frank and some people hated him. I did both, and I did them with everything I had in me. I ran into Joel Monahans in front of the theater in town a few weeks after he'd come back, and he told me Frank had come back able to drink more than any man he'd ever seen. "I think you oughta watch him, Travis," he said. "Or get someone else to if it ain't all right for you to be doing it. There's some nights when I don't know what he's gonna do. You know what happened to him in Nashville? He used to be a good singer."

"He won't talk about it with nobody, least of all me," I said. "Somebody wants to do something their whole life and they go to do it and then ain't good enough."

Joel's eyes were hooded in the noon sun. It was fall, getting on down towards Daylight Savings and the atmosphere seemed thin, like the sun and sky both were closer to us. "Oh, shit Travis. You know well as I do he's always been like this. Since he was young. You know what I mean." And Joel had fixed me with that special glare, the one that says I know secrets and we don't even have to say them out loud.

"Travis, it's a shame you don't come down here no more. I hope you don't have to come down here because of that brother of yours, but I'm afraid that's what's gonna happen if you don't get a hold on him."

After that talk with Joel I started thinking about Iron Mountain all the time. I decided to go back up on the trail Frank and I had been up that night and realized I hadn't been near those woods in almost twenty years. Strange how there can be so many places a person won't go in a town so small.

When I got there, the damned trail was so familiar to me I broke out in a cold sweat. The bugs weren't as thick as they would have been in July, but they were still there. As I walked, I saw pockets of the brush trampled down and scattered with beer cans, potato chip bags, and condoms. If I turned to my right I knew I would come to a bluff that overlooked the river as it started to bend. The Devil's Looking Glass, a sheer black rock face, overlooked the water on the other side. The black rock was littered with graffiti—God knows how they got up there—anarchy signs, and pentagrams, and 666.

Instead of turning towards the river I kept going up the mountain, past countless teenager hovels and the collapsed shanties of the old drunks that lived there. There's so much land that there's no way to police all of it. So much of it has to stay secret. The teenagers and old men know it. And me and Frank knew it, too.

I let the wild branches slap me in the face as I got nearer to the top. The trail had all but disappeared. I knew there must have been other, even smaller ones, all around me. I wanted to tear my badge off. I hated everything about the uniform all of a sudden, that I was a man who wrote tickets and put people in that little county jail. Not even really criminals most of them, just petty thieves and drunks, and the worst of them a murderer who tore the face off a young boy when he was driving wrecked out of his mind. The real crimes—the fathers beating their families, fucking around with their kids, the quiet murders—the town conspired around to keep secret, as if they were a part of how everything had always been. They were whispered about around the dinner table, over the Bibles on the back porch, the reeking spit cups, and raw cemetery earth.

There were times when I was damn sure everyone knew what me and Frank had done. After that boy came down out of the mountains, half dead and covered in blood and leaves, with his arm fucked up where some animal had started to gnaw on him. It was that animal that sent him up out of the of foot dirt we'd buried him in. All that got passed around like it was in the newspaper, even though the boy wouldn't say a word.

Those people might have known our names, might have passed them around every night like we were football heroes. I'm not sure what was looking out for us, but we could've murdered that boy—and we thought we had—and no one would have ever come for us. I sometimes wonder if they do know my name and now expect me to protect them as they've protected me all these years.

I got up to the top of the mountain. Pieces of the sparkly soft limestone this place is famous for glinted in the sun. They were scattered across the flat top like they'd come from a rockslide, but there was nowhere for them to come from. The ground was stained brownish or red in many places. The mountaintop can only be reached by walking, so it only gets a special kind of traffic. Frank must have known that, but I didn't. The whole time he worked on that boy I stood watching the dark of the woods, expecting I don't know what to come up out of them. He had that boy bent over a rock with rags and rocks stuffed in his mouth so he wouldn't make any noise. He was still and growled like an animal, his hands raked halfway up his back and tied with a piece of barn twine that smelled like dirt and tobacco juice.

The boy had a name. Luke Bloom. A faggot name. I was used to seeing him get his ass kicked in the hallway. He did swish, but I never wanted to hurt him. I never wanted to help him either. More than anything, I just wanted that fucker to disappear.

I've never forgotten his face after Frank was done with him. I wonder if I'll ever tell this story to another living soul. The versions passed over those country dinner tables might be good enough. Frank had tried to get me to fuck him and when I wouldn't, made me swing at him. He yelled so loud I was afraid all the people in the woods would come up and see what the fuck we were doing. Frank lifted him up and so I could punch him. He had to tilt him back so his head would stay up. His face looked like a burned tomato, mashed in and peeling and black. Even his eyes had blood swimming around in them. I don't think he saw me, even though he was staring right at me.

I drew back my arm just to get Frank to stop screaming, and the silence was merciful. Then Luke took a breath through that awful, mashed up nose, and I just wanted the noise to stop again. I punched him in the face and it felt like punching ripe fruit. I felt disgusting, like I'd pulled my hand back covered in maggots. And I punched him again and again, until when I came to I was out of breath and spattered with black up to my elbows.

"C'mon," Frank had said. "We gotta bury this fucker." He let the body drop, and I was sure the boy was dead. I wanted to jump off the bluff, just to get the fucking blood off of me in the river.

We wrapped him up in a big burlap sack our daddy used to pull moss in. I opened it up and it smelled like those awful early mornings that I went out with him and the branches were still dew wet and slapped against my face, and the wriggling sightless worms and black beetles and pill bugs clung to the underside of the moss. He didn't fit all the way, so Frank tied the bag around his knees. We carried him partway down the mountain and dug with our hands. We couldn't really see anything, but the ground was soft and wet. We dug until my hands ached and bled, and it was just enough to put him in the ground and cover him up a little. We finished the job with leaves and trash, anything we could find to hide the bare, dark dirt.

I thought about everything Joel Monahans had said and what happened on Iron Mountain the night I finally did get called down to Chucky's.

I had a feeling it was about Frank as I drove down there. I wondered what I'd do when I got there, if I'd be able to save him. If I'd want to. I felt light and sick, like when I got to Chucky's I might find Frank holding some kid's mashed face and telling me to hit him while the whole town watched and whispered. I swallowed back a mouthful of bile and flipped on the siren, gunning it over the gravel path, down towards where the road hugs the river. Big branches cracked under the bucking car but I still felt late.

I got there just a few seconds before the ambulance did. It felt like panic in the parking lot. There was a boy with a broken skull, blood leaking out of his head and across the wood plank floor. He had blonde hair. He looked to be about twenty.

"This was Frank?" I asked.

Joel nodded. "Yup. He took off headed east in that old van a his. Maybe you can get him. I'd say he started out ten minutes ago."

I didn't let myself think of the look of that boy's broke skull and dark blood in the moonlight. I jumped in my patrol car and headed up the road towards where the Appalachians get wilder and wilder and you could never conceive of the plains or the sea.

Going up those Iron Mountain roads made me think of the time I saw Luke Bloom after we thought we'd killed him. I read in the paper that he was still alive before I saw him. The paper said something had happened to his brain, that he had some kind of selective amnesia. I thought that he figured if he gave our names Frank would find a way to kill him for sure.

He was walking up Love Street like any other guy the day I finally saw him. School had let out and Frank had disappeared off to Nashville; I was going in to my junior year. It was midsummer afternoon, that dead time between two and four PM. The streets crawled. The yards were luminous. And nothing else moved, except for me and Luke Bloom.

We walked right toward each other on the same side of the sidewalk, the weeds growing out of the cracks of it as dead and dry as cemetery grass. Luke walked with his head down. As he got closer, I looked at his arm for that gnawed place I'd heard about. I couldn't help myself. It was easier to look at that than what we had done to his face. His arm was twisted and chewed up and bright pink.

The air became stiller and stiller. The Elms café across the street gave off the heavy, wet smell of sewage and discarded grease. Luke kept walking, and I noticed he favored his left leg over the other. When he finally raised his head, his eyes looked like a room with no light on. He looked at me and then through me. For a second he made me the ghost, and the whine of the hot summer insects pierced my eardrums. He walked right past me like he didn't see me. And then I thought, but I'll never be sure, that he made a kissing noise at me, his lips pursed together, from on down the sidewalk.

I came up on Frank's taillights after gunning for a few minutes. The road was so empty. We were head-ing into Carolina, past Flag Pond where the trash lived, somewhere near but incredibly far away from the interstate. I flipped on my sirens when I saw him, and he hit the gas. I knew where my brother was headed, up toward those high pines where he could feel like he was on top of the world.

We drove faster and farther and the roads climbed up and up. It felt like chasing an animal and not understanding that little dark spot in you that made you want it to die. I knew what the cedar trees would smell like if I stopped in the darkness, knew what it would be like to stand up top where the ground is swept bare and covered by rocks. The highest you can get to the sky around here, and we were coming up on it soon, together.

I couldn't imagine racing down the hill after him, even as I drove. I heard the horns of the logging trucks as they came screaming down, the big loads barreling them over the tight curves. I could see myself putting that gun up against his cheek as he slept, and I let the car slow on the uphill. I let him think he was winning. I could almost feel my car going backwards as we got near the top.

STATE TROOPER

I've been driving for three days. I took my best friend's car and I can still smell him in it.

I met Tallahassee one night when I was walking around in the neighborhood one of my cousins lived in, one of those places where the houses are small and smell like cats and wood smoke. There were cats everywhere, running all over the streets, living up under the houses, crying and going wild. It had just stopped raining and everything was still damp. The sky was yellow and purple running into each other, orange and dark blue around the edges.

There were other guys there, but it's Tallahassee I keep seeing, the way he caught the rail and leaned up when he saw me coming down the street. "Hey, get your ass over here and have a drink! I ain't seen you in ages!" When I got closer and he figured out he didn't know me at all, he laughed and gave me a beer anyway. He sat back and I said my name to Andrew and Rich and sat down in a patent-leather chair one of them pulled up. It was the kind you'd sit on at a hamburger joint. I sat there until Tallahassee's momma came out and ran us off, her hair done up in rollers.

I've been dodging the cops and tonight's the night they think they're finally going to get me. That damned pig done flipped his switch and is coming down behind me, flashing red and blue and white, just like the goddamned flag. He's probably got his little badge pinned gold to his shirt, and another one hiding like a wild card in his wallet.

Those lights are eating up the darkness, making it into something artificial. I put my foot down on the pedal and take my hands off the wheel. The wheels head towards that white line and the feeling is Jesus Christ, yes! before I clap my hands back down on it. Driving is like visiting ghosts. The road you ride over says something about everything that's ever been on it, but there's no real history. The road can't move and it can't talk to you, just like some ghost that's been trapped and is knockin around an old house. The best it can do is hold up a big black mirror and let you see what you can find there. You can drive over it and make up stories, but you can't pretend to really know what happened.

Memory works different out here. I can see every-thing that's held up in that big black; I see it over and over again, refineries pumping out smoke and steam behind it. The past just won't get dead and the gun in my passenger seat almost wants to say I'm sorry, but it don't.

There was one night before I left that I ended up flat on the pavement with a train roaring by. Tallahassee liked to park his car on the railroad tracks and play chicken with the trains. The car was his—he'd bought it off some old guy that had it up in his yard on blocks when he was sixteen—and he did whatever crazy thing he wanted with it. The worst thing that happened to it from him doing that was once the back fender got sheared off. The train had just barely nicked it.

I'd been running around with them for a couple of weeks when he pulled that with me in the car. It was in a place I used to walk over everyday when I was in school. It was fall, but it wasn't cold. The air just felt good, like something was going to change but you weren't sure how. We heard a train rumbling just as soon as Tallahassee killed the engine. In a minute or two I saw it bigger and blacker than the sky, coming right at us. I bet it was kicking up thousands of leaves. I jumped out of the car when it started getting close and instead of running I jumped up on the roof and started yelling at that train. This whistle started shrieking and I couldn't even hear myself. The train light was blaring right in my eyes.

I felt close to the stars standing on top of that car. The air smelled like dry leaves and exhaust and that oily, dusty, dark smell trains have. The air was electric with fear, too, coming out of my own body and the guys in the car. That seems like a long time ago now, jumping up on that car and wishing I was a ghost, the smell of dead leaves and summer in my nose, and those guys in the car, scared shitless, not knowing what to do. It's those few seconds I was in the air after they hit the gas that I keep seeing while I'm driving, just as clear as an orange leaf twisting in the streetlight. There was no time to be afraid before I landed on my ass and skinned everything off the heels of my hands. I was laughing when the train passed and they were still there on the other side, waiting for me.

I hated those fucking small-town boys for trying to get away from their lives by pretending they didn't care about them. I wanted to show them how it looks if you're not pretending, if you really didn't fucking care. I stomped up and down on the roof. After it was all over, I thought Tallahassee would kill me for leaving marks in the paint. I told him just to be glad I didn't get killed. He made like he was going to punch me in the mouth, but he didn't.

And I must have scared them. Andrew told me later that Tallahassee wasn't going to start the car. Andrew said his hands were lying in his lap and that he had to reach over from the passenger side and turn the key. *I even had to lean over his knees and push on the gas with my hands*, he'd said. As far as I know, Tallahassee never parked on the tracks again.

These last couple days on the road the factories have been keeping me company. They glow orange, gold, and white, and that gets all mixed in with the purple and black going on in the sky. They look like their own kind of ghost, long pipes and compressors and smokestacks pumping out vapor and by-products. They don't look the same during the day. They're just gray, and you can't imagine people in them, standing in lines, doing the same thing over and over again every hour. They look like they run themselves.

The yellow lights of the factories don't look like god. They're more like a puzzle you've got to look at again and again before figuring out what the fuck it means. They sit there like they've always been there, cars pulling up to them everyday, people punching in and out. But somehow it's the things that don't get used anymore, the big cranes and iron train bridges over wetlands, the abandoned warehouses with broken windows that show the setting sun, that are the things that make me want to stop, that feel like something I could put my whole life into. It must drive some people crazy, trying to figure out what kind of mess of engineers thought all this up and then let it die, but it makes sense to me.

I could get off at the next exit to lose this fucker, just blaze through the tollbooth and down a thin dark highway, and find some lost place in the trees to cut my lights and hide. I could get rid of him that way. That toll collector wouldn't show too much surprise when I roared through there. I've seen so many of their faces getting on and off the Turnpike, pale in the middle of the night under the fluorescents. They look soft and full of anger at the same time, like looking into the darkness and oncoming lights all night has done something to their brain. I always think about fucking with them to see what would happen but then I stop myself. They must be like pressure cookers, all that time to think and nowhere to put it. Their faces look like those saps getting off of work in my hometown. Sometimes me and Tallahassee and everyone else would be parked drinking beer in a gravel lot across from the Ford plant when they got off. I wondered if those poor bastards looked like that all day long, or just at the end of it.

It felt good to leave that little town, to get away from the cheap clapboard houses and shitty used cars, the kids running around their parents' little squares of yards, the little bit of rush hour that happened around five o'clock when all the factories let out. I drove around to some other small towns in Jersey and they were all the same, except the beach towns smelled like ocean spray instead of factory stench or exhaust. I went around to where I didn't know any of the kids running around on the bare yards, or what their daddies did for a living. I went where I thought there was no history, but it kept creeping back. Not in people, but maybe in words or a smell, a song I'd hear on the radio.

When I left after that robbery and said goodbye and fuck you all at the same time, all I wanted to do was go to the beach. That's what we were going to do that night, before we'd stopped in to get something to eat. I just couldn't stand it anymore, how I'd started to hate everything about those fuckers. Maybe this guy behind me hates everything about the men in his life, those fuckers down at the station or wherever it is they put em, those guys they bring in reeking of booze or with dried blood on their knuckles. I wonder if this guy is so far gone he hates the ones that ain't even around any more, like the poor fucker I passed last night wrapped in a sheet laying out on the highway, stopping up traffic and bleeding from jumping off the overpass. And those goddamn cops, just standing around and waiting for the coroner to arrive. Those fucks are beyond tears.

The ocean at night is darker than the highway. I wanted to drive all the way across it. If I could get a half-mile out in all that darkness, maybe that would be enough. I don't want to go forever, but I do want to find out what it is at the very bottom of me.

The things I always saw on the beaches were teenagers and the old teeth of fences in the sand. At night they moved underneath the piers and board-walks. They picked fights or drank beer or fucked in the sand. Close to the water you can't hear them, just get a flash of their mouths and arms and legs and the crash crash crash of the water where their goddamns should've been. That kind of desire seems like a red-hot coin, like something that would just burn up in your pocket, like something that would keep the sun coming up everyday. I feel it sometimes when I watch them, and I can't decide if it lasts for-ever or just for a few minutes at a time.

When I sleep on the beach and the early-morning sun comes up it makes me feel naked, like I can fool myself with all that darkness at night, and then it comes up to burn away everything I think I know. When I'm driving there's a few minutes when the red ball of the sun starts to rise, and it brights out every-thing else: the factories, the big oil cans, even the tips of the grass on the wetlands, and this is when the world makes the most sense. It's bright white and I can't see anything. I could run off the road; I could just let it burn out my eyes. And then it starts to move up the sky again, and I remember that things are the same as the day before.

When I watched those teenagers, I thought more of the guys back in my hometown. The ones that ain't ever leaving. The ones that carve some stupid, meaningless space out of a few thousand people and think they can live in it without dying.

There was that night we got jumped at the quarry. That happened right before I left them standing in that roadside diner. I didn't feel bad about robbing the place, but when I saw Tallahassee run out into the parking lot I almost wished I hadn't taken his car. He had a look on his face, like he wanted to come with me. The car might even belong to both of us now.

We were driving by the quarry and saw the Mustang that belonged to a guy who had fucked with Tallahassee. We stopped and heard people splashing and talking down below. They were swimming. Tallahassee killed the lights and engines and motioned for us to be silent. He got out of the car and took a baseball bat out of the trunk. I pulled my knife out of my hip pocket and started working on their tires. It wouldn't take no time, but I did it slow, giving the rubber a lot of small cuts, like I was spelling something out. When I stepped away I saw Tallahassee with that baseball bat. As soon as I got out of the way he cracked it up against the side window. Little silver shards of glass sparkled on the black seat cover.

The way he moved spread to us and started burning like wildfire. Andrew grabbed the tire iron out of our trunk and I grabbed a hunk of tree branch and we all started fucking up that car. He jumped up on the hood of the car and got the windshield out in three big swings and then he started jumping up and down, kicking out the shards of glass left hanging. We all started lighting up, kicking at that car and screaming right along with him. And it felt good to forget, to get up beyond a place that feels like death, to speak in a forgotten language. I felt just like I did when I got on top of the car in front of the train, like nothing could touch me but even if it did it wouldn't matter.

I was still feeling like that, black and untouchable as the space between stars, when I felt something hard and sharp pressed up against the soft cotton of my shirt. The guys who had been swimming had heard us and had come up the bank. One of their knives was right between two of my ribs. I stopped what I was doing, and I wanted to live so bad right then and I didn't care all at the same time. I had splinters working their way into my palms and I was covered with sweat and I felt just as hard as the stars. That feels like now, those lights closer and closer behind me, lighting up the dash, the music turned up loud, that same place most people are never able to get to. If this pig behind me catches up to me, he's gonna know what that feels like, too. I'm going to turn it on him and show him. I'm gonna make him see what he really cares about in this world.

There's too much wanting in the world. Too much wanting and never getting. The night I left seems like it goes on forever, and that same itchy thing that made me leave won't get out of me. It's like that feeling when I open my eyes and turn back the wheel, and every time I get too close it disappears. And it makes me wonder if they're like two sides of the same shiny coin, the white hot desire just before leaving and the hot air after that just keeps you moving.

There's a big red Hess sign on the highway burning bright in the dark. The wind is high and smoke from one of the nearby factories covers it, making it glow just like the devil. The big oilcans across the highway are lit by huge white lights. The tiny stairs that wind up the side of them have no shadows until that strobe light behind me hits them. Out in the wide expanse, I can see the lines of telephone wires and the big wooden crosses they're strung up on. The orange moon up above it looks like it's been streaked with oil.

I've got the radio up loud, but all I'm getting is gospel stations. Preachers yelling out to the refineries' glow about salvation, about the long lost, about some river of blood. I leave the dial and just listen, but damned if I can understand what most people are trying so hard to be saved from.

The radio relay towers blink red up and down in the distance. They ain't touched by the thing that's behind me. I don't feel scared, but I do know what fear is. Most people will try anything to get rid of the awful stink of it. That's the smell that rolled off most people in every town I've ever been in. It made me sick, like smelling meat frying on a hot day. Some people walked like death had em on a collar and didn't even know it. They wouldn't know what color the sky was if you asked them. Fear is a big sword that cuts down everything in its path.

Time ain't no straight line anymore. I got my foot down to the floor. Everything's just as crisscrossed as all the radio signals flying through the air. Those red white and blue lights are after me, the preacher turned up, hollering about Jesus Christ Almighty, the sky big and silent, air crowding in closer and closer, the sound of sirens speeding over and around the radio waves. I feel real mean, and loneliness doesn't seem like a dream, it seems real, something that comes in rotten on the summer air, or freezes the heart in winter. Or maybe this thing ain't mean, and I wonder who this man is chasing me, with his stuffed wallet and badge. I want to tell him what it's like to make a hole right in the center of yourself just to see if you can find anything worth filling it back up with. What he's got don't scare me, because the thing I've got knows all about him.

I close my eyes and take my hands off the steering wheel and I stop wanting to be saved. The darkness ain't smooth; it's all broken up by the lights behind me. I think about that Hess sign disappearing behind me, shining like the devil, and the look in that boy's eyes when I came at him even though he had a knife in my ribs. I turn the gospel as high as it will go to drown out the sirens, but I can still hear them.

USED CARS

They drove on an unmarked road that was little more than worn out gauges in the mud running through a stretch of woods Christine and Bobby had never been in before. Looking out the window made Christine feel like she was in a nightmare, the heavy branches sloughing alongside the car and making loud muffled noises, like insects scratching against her eardrums. It had rained the night before and the woods were almost luminous with the heavy wet branches, here and there blotted by yellow sun, and closer to the ground, plunged into a sparkling darkness.

Christine squealed when Bobby dug his fingers into her ribs from across the backseat. Gina Remington turned and thrust her bony arm into the shadowy backseat to wrench his hand away. "Bobby, what the hell you doing to your sister?" Christine screamed half-laughter and half-horror at the sharp cheekbones rising from the dark hollows of her mother's face as she grabbed Bobby's hands and pushed the two of them apart.

"Momma, wouldn't doing nothing to her!" Bobby sulked as he shot Christine a mean grin.

"Both you need to shut the fuck up," Stephen Remington said, his big blue-knuckled hands covering the steering wheel. "I can't think about driving on this blessed dirt track with the two of you making so much noise."

Christine's giggles faded to hiccups as she lay against the vibrating door, her hand gripping the shiny metal handle, amazed that for a moment her mother's face had looked like the faces shifting and disappearing on the rough skins of the trees that surrounded the dim road they drove on.

There were places where the woods became less dense, and the children noticed husks of trailers slowly being overrun by weeds and vines and the deep shadows of the trees where yards must have once been. The metal exteriors ran with rust like gauze stained with an old injury and the windows in many of them were completely dark, like the sticky black of an eye that has been gouged out. Christine felt the darkness behind those windows reverberate in her chest, in that secret place where memory creates history. She wondered what had happened to the people who used to live in those houses. She looked over at Bobby in the gloom of the car and he smirked at her, as if he'd seen what she had but refused to be afraid.

Stephen hunched further over the wide metal steering wheel. Gina sat straight up beside him, scanning the dense wet foliage out her window. The thick glass was smeared with silver gray swatches of left-over rain and the luminous green of the brush that crowded the road. Stephen swore as he slowed then stopped, sometimes cutting on the windshield wipers. "We should have walked," Gina said. He said nothing.

Neither child understood how old their father was. He was hard and tan, like something that had been fired in a kiln, but he did not seem worn in the same way their mother did. The cold fire of his eyes and the crags around them seemed timeless and powerful, as if he was slowly being weathered by a hard wind. Their mother was far more brittle, her face and hands like the broken slate sidewalks in their neighborhood. She looked like something that could be easily shattered by the thick tree roots around them.

Stephen had told the children they were going to look for gold when they started the drive. Both of them imagined running little pans of rocks through cold, clear creeks and looking for the hopeful flecks of gold like they'd seen in westerns. Christine knew that gold was wonderful and that people would kill each other for it, and she knew she must never tell anyone if they found it. They never saw gold on those trips and their daddy never let them get out of the car. When they were older, Bobby realized the big plants they brought home from those trips were other people's marijuana plants growing in the woods.

A few weeks after that trip, they drove home from one of their frequent visits to car lots in something different than what they'd arrived in. Stephen bought the two children ice cream cones from a drive-in on the way home and they ate them slowly before exploring the unfamiliar terrain of the new back seat. They mapped out their territories on vinyl that was a cool powder blue. The back seat made everything seem new to Christine, even the swirls of vanilla soft serve and the familiar faded Coke sign of the restaurant.

Christine touched her finger to the chalky gray dust of cigarette ashes left over in the metal lip of ashtray on the back of her father's seat and smeared it across the vinyl, surprised at how well the gray ash disappeared into the blue. Bobby's fingers went immediately to the places where cigarettes had melted the plastic and set about ripping them apart. By the time that car was traded in, the holes would be huge, showing the spongy foam beneath.

She sat up tall and looked at the top of her head in the rearview mirror, marveling at the dark hair and fading summer tan. Her dad liked to say she was dark as an Indian. The houses in their neighborhood looked smaller and more crooked than usual; the smell of smoke curling from a few chimneys made her mouth water.

Bobby hated the gray of the sky and the stray cats whose matted fur was wet with rain. He scowled out the window and drove his finger deeper into the cigarette hole on the back seat nearest him. Because he was older, Bobby knew the new car would be like a dream that lasted for only a few days. He closed his eyes and still saw the sun beating down on the windows and metal of the cars lined up in rows on the lot, so bright it felt like someone was putting something sharp right against his eye. The sparkles everywhere looked like the gold their father promised and could never seem to find.

Christine didn't know on the ride home that the torturous visits to the car lots would never end. Only a few weeks after the new car was brought home, Stephen wanted to go back to the lots on the weekend; just to look, he said. He walked through the rows of cars with his family behind him, cupping his hands and looking into windows, talking to himself, yanking at Gina's elbow every now and then. Sometimes the salesmen ignored them and other times they came up and wouldn't leave them alone, big gleaming smiles and voices like their throats were greased with oil. Stephen acted like he was ready to pull out his wallet and pay for something with cash, even if Gina was feeding them on peanut butter for lunch that week.

Some of those salesmen would get down and look Christine straight in the face with their big smiles and mouthwash breath, trying to show her dad that they knew what it was like to be a family man. They could make her skin turn cold on the hottest day. She often ran away when they did that, and grabbed for her momma's hand, wherever she was, squinting into the distance. Some Saturdays after they visited lot after lot, she would get tired and hide in the shadows between the cars. She imagined it was like being in the middle of the desert and finding a flat rock to curl up under.

Gina Remington hated the visits to the car lots. While Christine and Bobby stood listening to their father talk to the salesmen, Gina, looking agitated and distant all at once, sometimes just wandered off and stood between cars, waiting for her husband to be done.

Some men will love a woman only so much as he sees that she's a part of him. As long as there's that one little part, he'll drag her around by it until she's half dead. But it takes a special kind of woman to let this happen. As she got older, Christine liked to think her mother had made herself hard and hollow inside, that she'd put out of her mind all the things she couldn't change, and had found a certain kind of peace in that. She moved with great deliberation and was like the heavy pilings in the heaving storm of their father's childish, discontent desires. Gina Remington never talked about what she wanted for herself.

Bobby knew this about his mother and he hated it. "She just stands around all the time," he said to Christine, "like she don't care what we get!"

They had been through the big station wagon, two Oldsmobiles, and the Nova when he said this. They were on the dark blue Mustang they never should have bought, the one they had gotten because their father had wanted it so bad.

"Well, it don't matter what we get, cause in a couple of days it won't be good enough for Dad, and then we're just going to have to live with it."

The cars haunted Stephen. They became alive, always moving in the back of his mind. Each imperfection that had seemed permissible when the car was new—a dented fender, a tear in the upholstery, the knocking noise that began in the engine only two weeks after it was purchased—grew until it invaded his dreams, until it seemed he could no longer live with it.

But when a car first came home with them, he would take whole days on the weekend to wash and wax it. He soaped it up and rinsed it off, the streaks of soap and sponge thrust wet and wrung from the bucket, the stream of water from the green hose triumphant. In those moments—shirttail untucked, pants spotted by the hose, the arc of water and rainbow around him—Christine thought he looked completely serene, as if that inner cacophony had been quieted. Sometimes he made her wash the tires with a small brush, and she went over the white stripe with it, always surprised when the brownish dirt came off and the stripe gleamed again. After the car dried, he rubbed wax on thick and white in the shade on the street. You can't wax a car with the sun beating down on it, he said to her over and over again.

When Christine was thirteen and Bobby had just turned sixteen, Stephen announced that they would buy a trailer and move to a different neighborhood. He sat in the old deep chair in the living room as he told them this, his work sweat still drying. The fans roaring in the windows made him talk louder.

"I hate those things," Bobby said.

Stephen scowled. "What's ours'll be ours, and that's all the matters. You want me to spend the rest of my life renting?"

Christine didn't mention it to her brother, but the place she had stored the memory of those car trips through the woods came back and chilled her. She did not want to be one of the wretched; she did not want to disappear in some dark place.

When they finally bought the trailer, fifty feet long by sixteen feet wide, Bobby learned what he had suspected and his mother had known: it was better to rent a house than own your own trailer. For the first few months they lived there, the chemical smell ("Smell don't last," the salesman said) coming out of the walls burned his nose until it started to get cooler. Christine thought about getting cancer and Bobby stayed gone more and more. He had a job at a grocery store and stayed out with his friends as much as he could.

There was no wonder the first time Christine stepped inside the place like there was with the first car ride home, no hope that it would take her some place she didn't already know. She had come to her destination, and she did not like it. When they moved into the trailer park both kids thought about the roads they never could have imagined before. They understood that some kind of possibilities were gone, like highways rubbed off of a map with an eraser. They would always wonder what the names of the hollowness would have been. They knew their parents would never be able to run from that place because they owned it, and so it owned them. She remembered that she had not seen the rusted hunks of cars where the driveways might have been, just those houses, abandoned, sinking into the earth. The cars were never there because, if the people got out, it was the cars that took them away.

There was a look that came over Bobby's face when he came into the house, something dark, but not like a cloud passing over, more like the dark shadows in woods, like something that has decided it will stay for a while. When Christine watched him, she realized she had become afraid of him since they had moved. When he was home he acted worse than their father, who could not bear to live inside the imperfections he had not noticed before.

One night when Stephen saw that look on his face, he got so mad he held him down and started rubbing one of his waxing rags on him. It was awful to have that smell in the house, mixed in with cooking smells from hours before and the terrible smell from the walls. His muscles started to shine and Stephen kept yelling at him. Watching it, Christine crammed her hands into her mouth and remembered that was the same big brother who used to push her out of the way to squeeze himself between mom and dad. Gina's face flashed from blank to broken to blank and then she walked out of the room.

Christine saw that the move changed her mother. Her delicate resolve seemed pierced by a deep sadness. She felt vaguely humiliated by the interior of the trailer and made small additions to it here and there. She exchanged the hideous orange curtains that had come as part of the furnished kitchen for pale yellow ones. She seemed to take comfort in those curtains and lingered long after the dishes were done in front of the sink, watching the sun come through them and slowly crawl across the counter as it set.

The older Christine got, the more her mother broke her heart. It happened over and over again. Once, in that quiet time after dinner, when her father had gone outside to drink beer and Bobby had disappeared with his friends, she stood at the edge of the kitchen and watched her mother watch nothing. Gina's hands lay at her sides still wet from the dishes. She turned a little to the side and Christine saw the muscles were completely relaxed, that she looked like she had been wiped white and smooth as a river-worn piece of quartz.

Christine made a move to leave, but her shoes squeaked on the linoleum. Gina turned and the blank look disappeared. The complicated shale lines came back. "What're you doing, honey?" she asked.

"Nothing momma. Just going to my room."

Her mother looked tired and sad, and her voice was tender. "Do you like this place, Christine?" she asked.

"What do you mean?"

"This place we're living in. Do you like it?

"Well, it's all right, I guess. It's not what I'd have if I got everything I wanted." She paused, looking closely at her mother's face. She'd never seen her look so open. "Do you like it, momma?"

"Not really, baby. But I don't want to imagine what else I *would* want. Wanting anything in this world is just a burden."

"What do you mean?" Christine asked, but she was terrified. Part of her wanted to go to her mother, and part of her wanted to run away and leave her in the horrible loneliness of parents whose children have deserted them.

"I mean, what we don't have is driving your father crazy. And we're going crazy right along with him."

Christine thought about Bobby and how much he acted like their father, always restless. His body and face had become harder, his jaw mirroring the straight line of their father's. His body was as dense and compact as the cinder block steps that stood at their front door. He sat on them sometimes, his elbows straight out propped up by his knees, smoking a cigarette before going into the house. He often slammed the door because the rust stains that had started on the aluminum made him angry. He was like lightning that flashes in the sky just a little and then fades, the air heavy with something that probably won't come.

Bobby threw wanting off of him like sparks and they settled on Christine, pricking her here and there. She wanted to tell him that she understood, that she felt it, too, even if it wasn't the same. Most teenagers throw off sparks like that, and that's what makes everyone watch them from the corner of their eye, to see what they're going to do.

Bobby's friends seemed powerful. There was something about them that caused even the old ladies on their old block to seem both afraid of them and to love them. They were a cliché no one got tired of running their eyes and tongues over. And they knew it, as much as they could guess what was being said about them, and as much as they could see what the stares aimed at them meant. Sometimes the gray eyes that stared at them looked like a storm, like the clash of two warring fronts, one carrying hot rain, the other cold wind.

In their old neighborhood, everyone had seemed aware of them when they were standing out front on a Saturday, the other boys stopping by to talk for a minute, the women taking their kids to the other side of the street, middle-aged men either looking at them mean or asking them about their cars, about what they were doing with themselves. Christine started to understand that those guys, standing around doing nothing in particular, being tough and vulgar and hiding parts of themselves they'd probably pour out all over the place if you offered to suck their dick; those guys were both the hope and the scourge of the people they'd grown up around.

Bobby's friends didn't like being in the trailer, either. It was the narrowness and the smell, their shoulders said, that got to them. They would have filled up the whole house, so they lingered on the edge of the lot, drinking beer with the scrub grass coming up around their shins. There was no yard, just a bare strip of dirt so powdery it was like hot chocolate mix.

As indifferently as they treated her, Christine thought about them all the time. She almost felt that she knew their hearts and could have touched them, because they seemed so laughable and tender, so self-conscious. She knew this was what her mother saw in them. Once when Bobby had disappeared for a few days, Christine snuck into his room and tried on his clothes. The jeans were far too long, but his leather jacket could've fit. Almost. She knew one day that it would, if she still wanted it.

After they'd lived in the trailer park for a while, it started to seem like there were hidden roads within it, like the ones they'd gone over when she was younger, except they weren't out in the open. Christine knew you couldn't exactly drive over them, but they were there if she stood still for just a minute. That was the secret, being able to close your eyes and envision where you would go.

She had been sitting under a pine tree at the south end of their trailer the first time she saw those roads. The tree was huge, and she was surprised it hadn't been cut down. It leaked resin and the ground around it was soft with orange pine needles. The shadow of it was deep and cool in the summer, like a part of the woods.

Bobby's friend Danny caught her at home alone under that tree, her bare feet dirty from the powdery ground. She was fourteen by then, old enough to throw off a certain kind of spark whether she knew how to back it up or not. He got out of the car and she almost got up and ran back into the house when she saw him.

Christine became very conscious of her body. She felt the urge to cover herself up, lock her hands to her elbows, but she didn't. She was tall and filled with tough muscle and her dark hair was messy. Her chest was small and her skin was almost as dark as the dirt from being outside all the time.

"Bobby around?" Danny asked. He got out of the car and stood there, his elbows on the open door.

Christine shook her head. Her throat had dried up. "No, he's gone. Don't know when he'll be back," she said.

It was quiet and hot that day. Everything stood still. It was strange because there was usually so much noise in the place that you couldn't hear yourself think. The only thing she could hear was a television, so distant she couldn't make out what was being said.

"Anybody home?" he asked and slammed his door. The sound caused a dog to start barking at the edge of the lot.

"Mom and Dad's gone," she said. She felt a chill run up her spine, a shudder like a child realizing she is alone at midnight. "Cept someone's always around here," she said. "Trailers are less than spitting distance."

"You talk like a boy," he said and walked up close to where she was sitting. He didn't have to go far. "And how you all stand to live like this, right on top of each other? This is like the way they do it in the middle of the city. You think this is why they've got so many fucking babies, from being so close together?"

She shrugged her shoulders to everything he said, but she sat up taller against the tree. The dead pine needles stuck into her thighs. Later she would have the imprints of them on her palms and the thick resin in her hair. She felt it when she went to brush it back from her face. He had made her mad.

"Where do you live?" she asked. She looked past him to his car. "You want something from us?"

He looked at her and narrowed his eyes, spread his legs a little further. "You'd go for a ride in that car, wouldn't you," he said, smiling. He wrapped his arms around himself and she saw the muscles flash familiar, like the yellow lights of a movie marquee.

Christine thought of what it would be like to touch his skin, and it made her feel old in a way she didn't understand. It reminded her of the thing her mother had said to her about wanting. Looking at her had made Christine feel so tired, and there was that same feeling with Danny, cutting across the unspoken thing running between them. She felt if she did touch him, like a ray of light crumbling something ancient, they would both turn to dust.

"You got a message you want me to give to my brother?" she said to him. But she was throwing out a message to him, saying she knew exactly what was going on between them without saying anything at all. He'd just have to find it, like the roads Christine knew were cut out all over the place, if you had sense enough to see them.

Christine would never know, but Danny would be killed in a machining accident not far from where he grew up when he was thirty-five. He would look almost exactly the same as he did at eighteen. She occasionally remembered that afternoon at her parent's house throughout her life, and the memory of it always felt like a secret that had risen to the surface of her and sank back to its dark place when he drove away. She would remember noticing his skin, how it was just as smooth as hers, even with the sweat and stubble darkening his upper lip. In her memory she was frozen staring at him, wondering if she would turn as dry and hard as her parents before it was over. It seemed everything had flashed in front of her, her whole life and death and everything that would happen in between. She wondered what hidden roads could be found in the way someone touches you and if she'd missed something awful and wonderful by not touching him.

Later that day after Danny had left, in the house before anyone had come home, Christine wondered if she and her brother would ever be able to talk about all of the things they'd ever wanted. She wandered from room to room, the sun setting in beams against the dark wood paneling, dust visible on the air, shifting, an entire galaxy of its own. She smelled the hot interior of the house, beer and sweat and smoke and the odor that comes from someone who wants the world but puts off everything. She understood the smell, like the fear stink of an animal about to die, of someone who sees beauty and feels bludgeoned by it.

That moment would rise and swell and stay with her forever, the way some memories from childhood do: the sourness of her brother's room, his disappointment, his rumpled bed, the unexpired want like a stifled breath. She sat down on his bed, the mattress sagging already, and put her feet in an old pair of his big sneakers. She sat in the hazy light of his bedroom for long minutes, her feet swimming, and realized that Danny had never answered her question. *Where do you live?*

OPEN ALL NIGHT

My girl Wanda's got one of those jobs that kills you. Waitressing, wiping up chicken grease and long smears of mashed potatoes, a lined pad stuck in her dirty apron pocket. She don't really let it get her down, though. She moves through the night shift like everything in every heart of the men who come in there hungry and tired or just out for the night belongs to her.

I met her one night running around with some boys, in Tallahassee's car going up and down Route 70. We went in there at two in the morning, starving, talking loud like we still had the wind blowing in our ears. She came up to our table and asked us what we wanted to order. Tommy's mouth flew open and he said some nasty thing to her. She raised an eyebrow, but she didn't skip a beat.

"I can take this apron off right now and wipe the parking lot with your ass. It's up to you. I'll give you a minute to decide," she said and looked around at us. "Do the rest of you know what you want?"

I opened up my heart right then and dumped all of it on the table—the noisy jangling parts, the quiet, papery parts—just like opening up a wallet and spilling everything out. I think she must have heard it and was used to hearing that sound. She looked at me and smiled, like she might have some interest in picking up what I'd left on the table and putting it in her own pocket.

I told Tommy to keep his mouth shut after she walked away. In a few minutes Wanda brought us our food. She smiled and leaned over me before she set my plate in front of me. Tommy had an awful look on his face, his eyes all crazy and narrow and sharp. He didn't eat anything.

When we got up to pay the bill, Wanda gave me her number written on a little piece of paper. She walked over to the counter with us to ring us up. While we were figuring out how much money each of us owed, Tommy pulled a gun out of his coat and pointed it at Wanda. "Who's ass you gonna wipe up now?"

Me and Tallahassee and Andrew took a step back from him. Everyone at the front of the restaurant froze, but the people in the back didn't even notice. They just kept on eating and talking loud. Half of them were drunk anyway; you could tell by the way they brought their forks up to their mouths.

Wanda opened her mouth like she was going to answer, but Tommy waved the gun at her and told her to empty the register before she could get anything out. When she handed him the paper bag of money she looked him right in the eyes instead of down the barrel of the gun.

I was waiting for someone to walk up behind Tommy and give him an elbow to the neck, but no one did. A full three minutes passed late on a Friday night and no drunks or truckers came in. After he stuffed the money in his jacket he turned to Tallahassee.

"Gimme your car keys," he said.

"You're fucking crazy if you think I'm giving you those keys," Tallahassee said.

Tommy's eyes almost disappeared, they got so mean. He pointed the gun at Tallahassee. "Just give me the fucking keys."

Tallahassee threw the keys at Tommy and they hit him in the chest. He caught them with one hand and then shot a hole in the floor. I don't know if he did it on purpose or not. Tallahassee jumped back and Tommy ran out the door. It wasn't two seconds before someone was calling the cops on the black rotary-dial on the wall.

Our first date she asked me if the four of us had split up the money afterwards. "Don't lie to me," she said. "I know you all had to be together on that one."

"Who put that idea in your head? The cops?"

"Sure the cops think it, but it's just common sense."

We were sitting outside of her apartment building in my momma's borrowed car. My dad had just gotten me a job at the place where he worked, and it'd be a few months before I'd have enough money to put down on my own.

"Well, it ain't true," I said. "I wish we'd split that money and I wish Tallahassee had his car back, but none of us have seen him since that night. I ain't seen nothing on the news about the cops picking him up either. He could be clear across the country by now. How much less would you think of me if we had've split that money?'

"Well, he didn't kill anybody." She paused for a minute. "To be honest, I'd think more of you if part of that money had been for you," she said and laughed. And then I threw my head back and laughed, too.

"You know that wasn't the first time I'd ever had a gun pulled on me, but it'd been a long time. Not since I was ten."

"Who pulled a gun at you when you were ten?" I asked.

"My dad. Who else would pull a gun on a kid? When your friend took that gun out, I wanted to tell him what he was doing had already been done, but I figured that might be a bad idea, so I kept my mouth shut."

I smiled at her because I knew she hadn't told me that story because she wanted me to feel sorry for her. I could tell she was done feeling sorry about it. She made me feel good and reckless, and it reminded me of the first time I'd ever met Tommy. He looked really young, with a bunch of hair bright like corn silk, but I figured he was older because of all the stories he told. There was something in him that made me want to be near him; you just hoped all the crazy shit he did would rub off on you.

I started to think he was a little crazy the night Tallahassee parked his car on the train tracks to play chicken, and instead of waiting for Tallahassee to hit the gas at the last second like he always did, Tommy jumped up on top of the car and started yelling. He sounded like a ghost up there howling. And when the train came boiling black down the tracks and Tallahassee finally did hit the gas, he went flying, but he didn't seem to care. He got back in the car grinning, his hands bleeding onto his jeans.

I started up the car and we drove to a roadhouse she wanted to go to, a speakeasy that was in a big converted barn off Highway 70. We turned up a dirt road that was completely black for about a mile and then lights started peeking up out of the trees. "It's just over there," she said.

The flattened field was scattered with gravel and full of cars and trucks and motorcycles. I looked at her in the moonlight. "How the hell you know about this place?" I asked.

"I don't even know anymore," she said. "Maybe an aunt or uncle took me. Might have even been my mom. I've been coming here since I was real little."

"You know a lot of folks who come here, then?"

"Yeah, pretty much everyone. These people are just about my whole life."

I wouldn't be old enough to drink in a real bar for another year, but I didn't tell her that. When we walked in she led me over to a booth and made me sit down. The place was thick with people and music and sawdust and the smell of sweat and dry, packed dirt. From where I was sitting I could see her standing at the bar picking up our beers. A guy with dark hair under a greasy mechanic's hat moved close to her and she stood for a minute talking to him, her hand on his shoulder. I'd never watched a woman laugh like that before. How her eyes crinkled up and she looked young and old at the same time.

She slid back into the bar and put our beers on the table. They were already sweating. It was hot in the barn, even with the big doors thrown open. There was an open space where people were dancing, and most of the heat was coming from them.

"So what happened to your friend? Do you think he's gonna come around anymore?" she asked.

I shrugged. "I don't know. He was always doing some crazy thing, but I don't think he did them because he wanted to be caught. Some people are like that."

She nodded. "Yeah, I got a cousin who goes in and out of jail all the time."

I took a drink of my beer. "I don't think he'll come back. He's got no place to come back to. I miss him, but we'd beat the shit out of him for what he did."

"What about that guy whose car he took? What's he doing?"

"He wants to kill him. He'd had that car since before he could drive. It's making him crazy to think he might not see it again."

A friend of Wanda's came and sat down with us. After I'd been introduced they started talking like I wasn't even there. Every few minutes people would come over and say hi to her, girls that were just as young as us who glanced over at me and then looked back at her quick. Some were women who were old enough to be our mothers, who squeezed into the booth and talked into her ear and I couldn't hear a word they were saying.

I kept looking at her and then looking around, looking back at her and going to get us more beer. I noticed the old women's frizzy hair in the smoke, their big rough knuckles red like they'd rubbed them over one of those old washboards. The old guys with skin like leather and the young ones, trying to get girls to dance. It was hard to believe that the one would turn into the other. I pretended I could see something gathering below the old wood planks that made up the ceiling of the barn, something that came from every person who was in there.

When we stepped out of the bar into the parking lot, the moon was full and the gravel in the parking lot was silver and gray at the same time. There was a couple groping up against an old white pickup truck that glowed in the light. Looking at the way those two were going about it, at their shoes, a pair of black boots half dusted gray and high heels, I wanted to just stand there and keep staring. Wanda grabbed my arm and we got into my momma's car.

"So if you thought I was part of that robbery why'd you want to come out with me?" I asked after we'd pulled out of there.

She laughed. "Cause even if you were part of it, you had sense enough to *not* be part of it," she said.

I nodded. "What happed to your father anyway?"

"He's dead. And about the only time I see my mom is if she turns up at that bar back there. She's a drunk."

"Ain't you afraid some of that's going to rub off on you?" I asked and pointed at the beer she had between her legs.

"I'm not afraid of it. I've seen what it can do to a person. I feel like I already know whatever secret it's got to offer, and I don't especially want it."

"Does it bother you that I'm driving drunk?"

She laughed. "You're not that drunk, or you wouldn't be asking me."

I told her about the job my dad had gotten me, as an assistant sheet metal mechanic. I spent most of the day unloading duct and cutting measured pieces of it with metal shears.

"How do you stand that job you've got?"

"Well how the fuck do you stand yours? All I gotta do is bring people their food and eat their shit and come home at night smelling like it."

"The shit or the food?" I asked, and we both laughed.

She took another drink of her beer. "The one thing I learned from my mother is that you can be anywhere, doing anything, and as long as you have a way to understand it, you'll be all right. As long as she had a bottle, wherever she was, she wasn't anywhere else, you know what I mean? If you've got that, then you can love anything. Or, if you don't love it, you'll at least start to understand something about it, and you'll hate it less."

We drove on in silence. The moon was still out, no clouds anywhere, and the road glowed like the dust on the work boots of the guy we'd seen pushing that girl against the car.

Some people think that going to work is like death. I guess maybe it is, signing away a third of your life every day of the week. I thought about Wanda all day the next Monday as I was carrying big pieces of duct to the mechanics to fit together. Instead of being pissed-off about being in the sun and the way the metal cut into my fingers, there were whole minutes where the motion and noise around me came together and felt peaceful. My lunch break came up so soon I was surprised to take it.

But there were days the work just drug on and on, and all I could think about was the time. The worst thing was when we go into an old place that was being renovated, and we'd have to tear out insulation and asbestos and God knows what else. Sometimes I thought about spending most of my time doing something I didn't like and I'd want to die.

Tommy came to me sometimes on those days and I understood why he'd left. I just didn't understand where he was going. But that's just how it is sometimes: you have to let almost everything go so you can keep some part of yourself. Sometimes the letting go hurts, and sometimes it feels just as good as whatever it is that comes in to take its place.

I'd been seeing Wanda for months before I knew I'd fallen in love with her. One night, a guy I worked with asked me why the hell I'd drive two hours each way to see a woman, and there it was. I had my own car by that time and I thought about telling him what the sun looked like coming up when I was coming home, a big red ball on the horizon. How I looked at it and wanted to shout God Almighty because of a new day that belonged to me.

I told him about the time we'd spent in the junk-yard instead. I'd passed it a few times before, always in the afternoon or at night when you'd never even know it was there, and it looked different in the early morning sun. I wanted to take her in there, in all that scrap and twisted up metal and rats' nests in the old seats. Wanted just to walk around until we found some place good to settle down in for a little while. That yard was so big you coulda gotten lost in it, tall stacks of big tractor tires and backseats hot and dry enough to want to sleep in for days, pieces of shrapnel that could cut your heart out.

"What the hell we doing?" she'd said when we pulled up to the yard. She'd just finished the chicken we'd gotten at some all-night place. The road map at her fingertips was greasy.

"I wanna take a walk," I said. "Ain't been to a junkyard since I was a kid."

The yard wasn't open yet so I took out the bolt cutters from my trunk and cut through part of the fence. I hoped there weren't any dogs.

We crawled in there, and like anytime you get on the other side of someplace you're not supposed to be, everything all of sudden looked different. The old car fenders were the hardest, sharpest things I'd ever seen. Engine blocks were stacked on each other, black and greasy, endless. "Why'd you wanna come here again?" she said.

And I smiled, the corners of all those machines spread out on the hill, turning to red rust. "I got a cousin who works for Ford. What do you think he'd say if he saw all this?" I asked.

She laughed and leaned up against one of the old cars. An old Chevy. "Unless your cousin's a goddamn idiot he knows this is where what he makes is gonna end up."

I went over and kissed her then and it hurt to close my eyes on her big brown ones, but I did. Everything went dark and I didn't mind it, with the way her lips felt and the sun still there even with my eyes closed.

We got in one of those lifeless old backseats and the morning got hotter and brighter. And for just a minute I could hear Tommy laughing before the big black of the train rolled by the night he climbed on the car, could see how his palms were bloody when he got back in. I heard the junkyard dogs barking somewhere in the distance, maybe getting close to us, shut up in the skeleton of that back seat, not caring about tomorrow or punching in the time clock or the way the sun kept inching up in the sky.

When we were done and back on the highway, the day didn't seem the same. She sat beside me, but I knew I'd have to drop her off again, and we'd have to go back to everything. Then I started to hate the way the sun moved. I just wanted to keep driving. It's different than the feeling I got when I drove around with my old friends, but those feelings have something to do with each other. This is bigger somehow, the kind of thing that makes you hurt and get bigger all at the same time. The kind of thing that mixes in with fear, and makes living feel like standing on the edge of a big cliff. You could fall off at anytime, but why would you?

I think Wanda must love me back. It fills up the car sometimes, gets so big it's stuck in our throats and won't let nothing but silence out. Sometimes when I pick her up late I'm listening to gospel. She laughs when I've got it on, says rock 'n' roll has all the religion that she needs. But it's not that I really believe in God, I tell her, it's that I like listening to people that believe in something. Everything's got religion in it, she says, and that's as close as we get to talking about it. She rolls down the window and puts her arm out into the daylight. And in the silence, we keep covering ground.

MY FATHER'S HOUSE

Caleb Wilson grew up in a place no one had a name for. He grew up as Cassandra, hair beneath the black and white of old photos the color of hay in winter. He sees that color hair in the mirror and in his memory when he shows the photos to friends. It is something he rarely does.

Caleb's family lived on something that was not quite a plain. There were small hills and misshapen breaks of pine trees that were bleached white and made one-sided by the wind. They were surrounded by emptiness and a big sky. Sometimes on the rare trips into town for groceries, shadows from fast moving clouds would overtake his father's mud flecked truck before moving on across the plain. Those shadows left thumbprints on his heart that he felt in his dreams after he moved away to Omaha.

Caleb's father left a heavier thumbprint after he left, a complicated smudge of memory like the deep grain of old polished wood. In Omaha he lived with two people who he imagined had uncomplicated dreams, who did not wake up in the middle of the night with deep grimaces of terror or a name that was not their own ringing in their ears. Sometimes his memories were too deep even for dreams and he awoke from utter darkness, still tired, as if he'd dragged himself freezing through the cedar groves in winter.

The dream that came back to him again and again was the one where he watched his father kill hogs. Caleb had slopped them when he was little, turning up the big buckets of scraps and feed and corn cobs into their trough.

"You have to be careful," his father said, "because they'll eat anything. Even you." He smiled when he said this, but it seemed they would, that if he fell into the mud they would burrow into the meat of his legs and stomach. Sometimes Caleb smelled their feed on the air at odd moments, ground up corn and barley with something sweeter and darker underneath it.

The hog he always dreamed of was the largest they had owned. The stiff hairs on his big belly were brushed with shit and his giant feet punched holes in the muck of the pen. Caleb stared at him as the pig snuffled at the slop and pushed the smaller pigs out of his way.

Caleb was watching from the edge of the field the day his father killed that hog. The sky was silvery instead of blue. The hog hung a couple of feet off the ground from a small crane. It had a darker third hole in the middle of its head the same size as its eyes. His dad cut its throat with a machete and let the blood run into the hard ground. The sound it made was like rain running out of a gutter.

Caleb wondered if his father knew he was watching. He stood off in the field so that his father had his back to him. He cut the pig down the middle and emptied its guts with his bare hands. When its intestines hit the ground, the smell of shit almost knocked Caleb down. They were gray and loose and made him think of the sea snakes his mom had shown him once in a book.

His father was covered in blood by the time it was over. It matted down the coarse hair on his arms. It wasn't the image of his father's blood covered arms that haunted Caleb so much as the smell of the inside of the hog, an odor so awful it was as if the animal had been carrying death around inside of it. He watched later as his father chopped it up in the smokehouse, the smooth dark of what must have been the liver being cut into even slices, and the edge of the cleaver disappearing into the gray chopping block. His father struggled to pull it out each time.

When Caleb moved to Omaha everything—the telephone poles, the cars, houses—filled his vision in such a way that it was hard for him to think. The empty streets late at night and the dark sky were a comfort to him, and once he realized he was looking for the empty expanse of the ranch between the things that made up the town, he began to understand that there is emptiness of all kinds, not just the wide-open empty of plains and big sky. Still, Caleb was afraid the vastness of heart that had been with him since he was young would be cut up, made less perfect by the density of the city streets that surrounded him.

This understanding had come to him first on the plains and later from books. Before Caleb was able to drive, they lived too far away for him to attend public school. He was home-schooled by his mother until he was a teenager. Once a month, a traveling library for rural people came around, and he took as many books as they would allow him. He took everything that was in them and put it inside of him. When he started thinking about what it would mean to be a girl who became a boy, he first conceived of it happening in those books, of how it would look unfolding on the pages. Would it be a good story? Would it be something anyone would believe?

His memory did not change when he started to change, even though he half expected it to, as if the shifting landscape of his body would affect the landscape of his mind. He had sensed this possibility in the small expanse of the cocoon of girlhood, and it seemed as large and wide as the country around him, until he began to feel stifled by the clinging web of the person he'd been born as.

His mother might have sensed these things about him, an uneasiness that she couldn't put her finger on. She sat with him out on the wide porch in good weather and taught him from books. When he was old enough to drive to the high school forty miles away, he missed those hours with her, the lessons interspersed with stories. She treated the lessons with reverence, and her kindness gave him a great love for them. He was thankful, for out in all that emptiness, even a little bit of discontent can destroy a person's heart.

On the trips to get supplies, they often passed abandoned houses out in the fields by the highway. Caleb became used to them, and watched their roofs cave in piece by piece, the walls turn in on themselves. He wondered who had left them or if the skeletons of an entire family would still be there if the old doors were pried open.

Seeing these things made him fearful as a young child. It came to him on the dark wind and found its way through the cracks of his window. He knew that it would be difficult for him to leave his father's house, that there was little money to send him to school. He saw himself rolling up and dying with no one to notice it, saw himself an old man even when he was a young girl, turning as dry and still as dead trees and old pieces of shingle.

Years later, after Caleb had transitioned and graduated from college, long after he was no longer a girl and no longer a boy, he decided that he must tell his father what had become of him. He had not seen him in many years. He did not know how to tell him other than to show him. He drove home to the westernmost edge of Nebraska in the small hatchback that he hated. He was much larger than when his father had last seen him. His shoulders were broader and the muscles on his arms had miraculously sculpted themselves. He wore jeans and heavy boots, a dark shirt that buttoned up over his smooth chest. Before he got out of the car he placed his cowboy hat carefully on his greased hair.

The lights in the house were burning brightly. They were jarring in the thick darkness, like lights switched on suddenly to bring someone out of sleep. Caleb saw his father in the kitchen, his dark hair grayer, standing over the stove. He slowly lifted a cup to his lips and stared out at the flash of headlights in his yard.

He believed and didn't believe that his father would be surprised. Masculinity was written in their history together. It was something that had always been with them, like the damp undershirts his father wore close to his skin. As he walked across the dry yard to the door, he thought of his mother's funeral ten years before. He had stood at her grave in a dress weeping, feeling like it was the only thing he could do to respect her.

When Caleb's father came onto the porch and saw what his daughter had become after ten years of absence, he seemed to see Caleb not as something dead, but as a big storm that you can see moving across the plains whole. A big storm that's going to destroy your house and wreck your crop and drive your animals mad. Caleb saw that his father had aged, his eyes hooded by drooping eyelids, his skin gray. The loneliness of the empty fields seemed to have twisted up inside of him.

Caleb's father looked at him kindly, until Caleb stepped fully into the light from the porch. He saw his father's eyes get wide and the big fists clench, and that spark of anger made him look much younger. The long, blunt fingernails bit into the flesh of his palms as his knuckles moved beneath the skin. Caleb had a flash of wondering if his father thought he looked like photos from when he was young.

"What the fuck have you done to yourself?" he growled.

Caleb did not know what to say. Everything that he had rehearsed had left him. The wind howled around them.

"This is the reason you haven't seen me in so many years," he finally said.

His father didn't say anything, but he moved more quickly than Caleb would have expected, turning in his big work boots on legs still thick with muscle. He drew up close to Caleb, whose words remained frozen in his throat, and punched him hard in the face. Caleb stared up at his father, blood running down his chin from a broken nose.

Caleb's father hit him until his face was bloody and swollen. It felt like his father was trying to erase some part of him. But Caleb's face looked so much like his that Caleb wondered if he was trying to erase some part of himself. He threw him onto the grass and threatened to kill him. Caleb ran when the bigger man came after him. He ran until the darkness had overtaken everything and he could no longer hear his father coming after him. The never-changing smell of the pines reached him even though his nose was filled with the copper of blood and shock.

His dark hours in the cedar grove felt like a strange culmination of his childhood, the blood running down his chin as thick and dark as the hog's blood boiling onto the ground. He pictured his father's huge arms, matted with black hair, the hands like thick claws, the fists familiar. His father had been handsome, but Caleb felt he had always known of the monster in him.

He hid in the pine break until the lights in the house had gone out and the plain was dark. He could hear nothing save for the wind. The memories locked in the deep smell of the cedar made the dead seem alive, the new like it had never existed. In those memories, Caleb does not become a boy. He does not remain a girl because he never was one. He is something there is no word for, for when he speaks out loud of himself, the words feel strange on his tongue. When he was a child, he slipped into his father's shirts, putting them on like a second skin and wondering what would happen if he could leave them on forever. They smelled of dust and horsehair, the sweet smell of open air and cow shit.

He limped back to his car and on the drive home understood simply and completely that he must make his own history. Caleb's dreams of his childhood stopped after his father beat him. He saw his past as a severed bridge over a large chasm, the boards disappearing into the crashing water below. He feared a similar disappearing for himself, feared that no one would know him as he knew himself. This loneliness stretched out and covered him, like the shadows of the clouds he remembered from childhood. A person's heart will pound for the things he thinks he has forgotten.

When Caleb was forty-five he moved back to the plains. He gave up the job he had teaching geology at the university in Omaha because he could not stop thinking of the land. He and a lover bought an old house that was distant from any town, but not as remote as where he had grown up. He fell in love with the house in the process of repairing it, and he and the lover spent long evenings on the porch after dinner watching the horizon grow dark all around them. He was comforted by the space and silence, and felt peaceful in a way he hadn't in the twenty-five years since he'd left his father's house.

Soon after the move his lover bought two horses, gray and black. Caleb repaired the fence of the old corral for their arrival and watched as his partner, a former rodeo rider, broke the mean gray horse in. It looked furious in the rising dust, but it also looked like it would enjoy giving up. Caleb leaned over the fence and pulled his hat down to shield his face against the sun. He stared carefully at the horse's eyes, and did not look at his lover. He was only a flurry of arms and boots and leather.

When the horse would allow itself to be easily ridden, the lover handed him the reins. "This horse is for you," he said, with the same tender, trembling tenor he used when he injected Caleb with hormones.

Some experiences are so far from universal that talking about them makes them seem even smaller. Caleb did not know how to describe the details of pulling the hormone, suspended and thick in oil, slowly into a syringe, and then injecting it deep into the muscle of his thigh. What could he have told his father or any of his lovers about his fear of visiting the doctor, his knowledge that he had undergone a metamorphosis that had made him an object of curiosity to anyone who knew? The words he had not been able to say to his father began to play again and again in his mind. They stuck in him like the long-gone white branches of a deadfall.

Caleb awoke one night in the darkness and understood his father would die. He had not dreamt of him in many years. In his dream he saw his father turning into one of those disappearing houses by the road they used to pass. Caleb parked his car on the narrow pavement and ran to it. He wanted to go to him, to light a fire bright enough to read by. The rough grass had not been cut in a few seasons. It brushed past his knees. Inside the darkness became almost complete, and Caleb thought he could hear his father's voice, the high rough Midwestern twang, asking him what his mother taught him that day, asking her to pass the butter. Caleb busted through what might have been the bedroom door and thought he heard his father yelling. The smell of the horses they used to keep, the first horses he had ever known, filled his nose. He looked out the window and the pines had been stripped of everything by the wind. They were like giant arrows pointing toward the sky.

He saw himself mouthing the words to explain his existence, all of the poetry he had never been able to speak aloud, but he could not hear or remember them. The walls of his father were dark, and it was he, finally, that was disappearing. Caleb sat soaked in sweat, the sheet gathered around his waist, in the darkness of the bedroom as his lover slept. He wondered if loneliness could eat away his heart until it showed on his face. He thought of going back to the ranch and finding his father again. He felt crazed and unmoored and was reminded of the sad, far-away look his father's horses would get in the win-tertime. He wondered how his new gray horse would take to the plains. He felt the awful arms of the trees rake across his heart and knew part of his dark blood would always belong to his father.

REASON TO BELIEVE

Kyle William Abel saw his father baptized when he was fourteen years old. It was in a country river, the red clay banks rising up on either side. The sun was on its way to setting and everything along the river— the black suits and white dresses of the congregation, the deep green trees and purple shadows—was touched with a red from the sky that almost matched the red of the river. His father's eyes stayed closed almost the entire time as the preacher prayed over him. He raised a white handkerchief and placed it over George Abel's mouth, his other arm raised towards the sky, his work tan glowing like copper. Kyle William saw his father's eyes flash open and be filled with the pink golden water at the last possible moment before his head was completely submerged. The preacher held him under for a moment, perhaps to make him think more carefully about his inevitable meeting with God, before pulling the handkerchief away from his father's mouth and waving it around, pink and wet, like a part of his heart. Kyle William's father shot up out of the water, his white shirt glowing not pink but a shadow of deep clay red, like blood that will not come out no matter how many times it has been washed.

George waded up out of the water and the congregation began to clap and sing. "Are you washed in the blood, in the blood, in the blood of the Lamb?" they sang in frenzied rounds, the women picking up strange high notes from some nasal place in their throats, the men pounding out the refrain from deep in their chests. The sun sank lower behind the hills so that the clay red light disappeared and was overtaken by the deep green purple shadows of the trees.

I reckon I am now, George thought, looking down at his chest and stomach showing through the wet white shirt. I'd look like a ghost out here in the dark, he thought, unsure of whether or not he should be singing with everyone else, or if the singing was just for him.

He looked over at Kyle William and wondered if the boy remembered being baptized. They had taken him to that very river and dipped him in it when he was just a few months old. "God will protect him from the black snakes and mosquitoes," the boy's mother had said. Kyle William screwed up his little face and started bawling so that he swallowed a healthy bit of the river water. The preacher could have sprinkled water on his near-bald head and that would have been just as good, but he'd submerged the entire baby's body instead. "That child will be so holy," he said afterwards, "for having swallowed that much of the River of Life."

Kyle William did not remember his baptism. He was terrified of the river and dreaded the day his mother and father would drag him into it. He hated the way the wet red clay sucked at the black of his shoe.

George was fifty-four years old. His face had become deeply lined, his kinky, black hair frosted with white. His rough hands were many colors—the hard walnut of his knuckles, the reddish fingernails with their pale half moons, the almost beige palms. Kyle William did not understand why, at the age of fifty-four and in the middle of June, his father finally chose to be baptized.

The next day Kyle William asked him about the baptism as they hoed under the hot red sun. Their hoe handles were rubbed dark and shiny where their hands held them each day. His father paused to mop up the sweat on his head with a red handkerchief.

"Did you see what it looked like under the river?" Kyle William said.

George stuffed the handkerchief into his back pocket. "It looked like red. I saw the sky and then I was under. There was that water full of grit and then I closed my eyes."

"Did it feel like anything?" Kyle William asked.

His father shrugged. "The water stopped up my ears, but I could still feel vibrations from out on the bank. There was a peacefulness under the water. I didn't want to come back as soon as the preacher brought me back up." He put his hoe under his chin. "I guess it felt like getting swept up in the River of Life, like I could've stayed there forever."

"But you knew you had to come back," Kyle William said.

"Yes," his father answered.

Kyle William thought of the way his father's eyes had stayed closed, the way he had thrashed when the preacher finally let him go, and continued raking the hoe through the tobacco plants.

Later that night George wondered if he had made a mistake by telling his son a lie about what he had felt in the water. He wondered if the river water of Kyle William's baptism had flooded the banks of his young son's heart and made it into something that he would never be able to understand. His own baptism had felt like looking at something that was dead and wishing it alive. He had expected to see the light of the Lord in the river, but what he had really wanted to see was the light of himself. He'd gotten a mouthful of dirty water instead. He was afraid, more than anything else, that Kyle William would grow up to be the kind of fool that puts too much faith in anything.

George's family never baptized their babies. They waited until a child knew enough of itself to choose to do it. The boy's mother had insisted they dip Kyle William right after he was born. "He's too young for it to mean anything," George had argued. "He won't even remember it." She slammed down her glass of ice water. "Some part of him will always remember it. He'll always be different. He'll be marked for the Lord. God will see it. He will know."

So they had baptized Kyle William and the boy's mother had wept. Looking at his son as they moved slowly through the field, he wondered again if the river had made his son wiser. He was startled for a moment, surprised by his own faith in the power of the water.

Kyle William was not scared of God, but of the things people did in His name, of the ways they contorted themselves around the idea of Him. He was scared he would never feel moved to go to the altar and offer his soul. He had first heard of hell not from his mother or father, but from a cousin, an older boy with close-cropped hair and thin, stringy muscles. They had stood in the woods one early fall, taking turns swinging on a big grapevine they would later learn was covered with poison oak. The leaves on the forest floor were newly fallen and crisp, but beneath them was the spongy, wet decay of years.

"It's like this lake of fire," he'd said, "that you git put in and can never git out of. My momma says they's people down there crying for a glass a ice water."

The high whine of an insect came from the bushes. It seemed to pierce his vocal chords, and his mouth suddenly filled with spit. "I don't see how you can burn forever," Kyle William said after thinking for a minute. "There wouldn't be anything left after awhile."

His older cousin knotted his forehead. "It's not your body that goes there, exactly," he said. "It's something else. It's like your ghost goes down there and you stay in the ground."

Kyle William puzzled over this, his hand under his chin. His cousin seemed to have forgotten what they were talking about.

"C'mon," he said. "It's your turn."

Kyle William walked with the vine up the bank. His feet slipped in the mud and old leaves and the roughness of the vine had started to rub his hands raw. Later it would turn into one of the worst infections the doctor had seen. He had to wrap his hands in gauze, tortured by the numb itching of them. The sun was hidden by thick gray clouds, so that a dull brightness showed through the bare branches of the trees.

He took a running go and pushed hard against the bank as it disappeared. His feet sank in a little and then he was sailing through the air. The rough, toxic bristles of the vine planted themselves further in this

146

hands and cheek, but he would not know it for another day. He landed badly and his knees sank into the wet of the forest floor. Above him, the gray sky yawned open, like a milky, sightless eye.

His fear of the altar had started when he saw his grandfather die. It was then he began to suspect no amount of praying would save him from what was coming. His grandfather had been a holy man, but he never went to church. His Bibles were falling apart. "You've got to find it on your own, or you'll never really understand what it is you do find," he had said more than once.

Kyle William's grandfather took him on long walks through the thick woods sometimes, their shoes silent on old beds of orange pine needles. His grandfather prayed in the woods, his wrinkled forehead pressed against the resiny bark of one of the big pines. Kyle William tried to memorize the words his grandfather muttered in the darkness of the woods so he could repeat them as he lay in bed, but he could never remember. His grandfather's ragged tone and garbled words were so different from the neat, quiet prayers his mother muttered every night on her knees in the living room that he wondered if the two things were related.

His grandfather had lived in a little shotgun house a few miles down the road Kyle William lived on. The yard was overgrown with wildflowers and blackberry brambles, save for a little square in the front that he kept trimmed. His grandfather had thrown out almost everything when his grandmother died. Inside, the house was almost bare of furniture and swept clean.

It had been high summer when he died. Kyle William walked into the house and his grandfather was lying face down on the floor. His stack of Bibles was knocked over and they lay scattered across the floor, their forked bookmarks like tongues. Their sour, quiet smell filled the hot air of the room. Kyle William dropped the jar of jelly he'd brought for his grandfather and it rolled across the floor. He uttered a high, thin shriek and ran out of the house.

He stood outside with his family the day his grandfather was buried. The lip of earth that surrounded the grave was made of thick black topsoil and hard red clay. The smell of the clay reminded him of the copper taste that rose in his throat when he worked too hard on cold days. The casket when he leaned close to it smelled faintly of bibles. When he looked in he saw that his grandfather was being buried with one of them, a black bible with pages so thin they were almost transparent, their outer edges dipped in red.

After his grandfather died, Kyle Williams began paying closer attention in church.

The heaviness in his heart begged for an explanation. He watched his mother sing in the choir, her hymnal spread open at her chest, her eyes open wide at the congregation. He wondered why she kept the hymnal open when she already knew the words.

When the preacher came to the pulpit red-eyed and tight-knuckled, he was the great swell that filled the emptiness. He seemed to animate the congregation with the force of his breath. His voice echoed from the roof. Women collapsed in tears. The men shouted and stomped, letting go in front of God. And each Sunday, at least one somebody went up to the altar and laid their soul bare.

The fury never touched Kyle William when he thought of going to the altar. He imagined the congregation staring at his back, looking past his skinny backbone and ribs to his heart. He knew that his hands and legs would shake, that his brains and lips would freeze when he knelt. He knew as he watched his mother sing that the pins and needles in his legs and the sting of the bristling red carpet would be more present than the spirit of the Lord. No space would open up for him. He would have nothing to say to God and everyone would stand as witness to it.

Kyle William knew his mother was worried about him. One day he had heard her talking with two of the ladies she sang with in the choir. Their voices carried through the screen of the kitchen door. He had been sitting out on the porch, sharpening the blade of a scythe with a whetstone for his father.

"Well, he is getting to be old enough. Might even be too old. After they git too old sometimes they start thinking they're too good for it."

"It's just as well he's waited a little, so he really knows what he's doing. Might be that's just how it runs with the men in your family," the other woman said, and he recognized the voice of Crinthy, a heavy-set woman who often came to visit his mother.

"Well, my boy got baptized and you see where he ended up."

Kyle William imagined the ladies nodding. He had often heard his mother speak this man's name in hushed tones, about what a shame it was that he ended up in Brushy Mountain Penitentiary.

His mother spoke, her voice sharp. "Oh, I believe it does good. I believe it does something to a body's character, whether they remember it or not. I believe it changes them."

"Well, do you think he's going to go to the altar anytime soon?" The woman with the convict son asked. "If he don't do it soon, you might have your proof right there. A baptism don't mean nothing if there's no feeling behind it. Do you think he really believes?"

Kyle William had not been able to hear what his mother said. He ran the stone across the metal until the blades were shiny silver and sharp enough to cut through the heavy squalls of tall grass that would dry into hay in the summer sun.

George Abel hated going to church. He had felt a terrible guilt in the years he did not go, but he had preferred to stay home and do extra work in the garden or make sure there was supper for Hazel and the boy when they got home. Death seemed closer to him with each passing day, and the tenor of his life was very bleak. He could hear it in the motor of the tractor and the sound of the blades scraping up the earth, the relentless caw caw caw of the crows overhead. It came to him even in the dinner dishes at night, the sounds of his wife Hazel washing and drying, the cacophony of clinks as she put them away. It even came on the flapping of the sheets she hung out to dry in the bright sun and in the frost that bit them in winter.

After becoming saved, he despised himself even more, but his contempt was not sharp; it didn't draw any new blood. The feeling was too deep for that, and it propelled him along evenly, like a car driving slowly through shallow water. The fields shrank and rose, and the lack of possibility mocked him. The Indian ghosts he had once imagined living in the woods no longer inhabited them. He sometimes stood at the edge of the woods after a day of work and peered into the coming darkness. Nothing was there, save the rustling of rabbits and squirrels and raccoons, and the occasional crash of their neighbors' brown cattle. The noises rose and disappeared and he stared off into the darkness, feeling himself going mad from the notion that nothing lay behind those sounds except for skin and muscle and fur. He searched the darkness until it stood out and separated, but the nothingness remained.

Hazel insisted they pray in the living room every night before bed. She knelt down in her dressing gown and he and Kyle William in their pajamas. She led the prayers without knowing it. Her voice swelled with a sound bigger than those things in the woods, and George and Kyle William followed her. They knew where the ebb and flow would be, where to insert a low Praise God!, how to quickly demure when Hazel began to trail off. Our Heavenly Father, Who art in Heaven, and in Jesus' Name… Amen. George tried each time to follow her words to the source that pushed them out but could not.

Why he had lied to Kyle William about his baptism came to him one night as they prayed. His voice rose with the prayer and tears stood out in his eyes. He saw the darkness of the surrounding woods, and the animal crashes within them. He felt himself swell up and wondered if he was about to be touched by the hand of God. He understood that the moment just after losing faith is the deepest and truest anyone will ever know. The truth was barren and hard and left room for only the most bitter, stripped joy and still it filled his heart.

In the days following his father's baptism, Kyle William noticed more of how his mother and father were different, how she seemed to spread dark jam onto biscuits in the morning with everything in her, while his father was constantly uneasy, tearing at the corners of his nails, distracted by something that neither of them could see. He wanted to ask if they were happy but knew he could not. He loved his mother but was often puzzled by her, that she seemed to be affected by the smallest things. "God made everything," she often said, "because He wants us to notice it all." She inhabited her own world, where everything was touched by the light of God.

Kyle William tried to understand this way of being and could not. His father moved through the world doggedly, with a grimness around his mouth that opposed the light step of his mother. Kyle William thought his father seemed very wise and his mother full of joy, and he could not decide which would be better for him. The question of the altar continued to plague him, and he sat stiff in church on Sunday beside his mother with a cold sweat between his shoulder blades. He felt cursed and wanted terribly to feel the hand of the Lord. He wondered what secrets his father's saving had given him, and if his mother loved him more fiercely than before, even if they did not seem touched by the same light.

They were working on the bottommost piece of land when Kyle William spoke to his father of the altar. The land was rich with the silt that stayed in the topsoil from when the creek overflowed. It was a gentle flood that happened almost every year. The sky above them was clear, the kind of clear expected in October, not in June. The creek threw off maddening darts of light.

Sweat ran down his forehead and stung his eye. He hated physical work with such a deep vehemence that sometimes it was easy to hate his mother and father for bringing him into it. He swore he wouldn't have to do it when he got older, but he had no idea how he would break away from it. He kept thinking of the vision of his father rising back up out of the water, the way he looked startled, like a child.

They sat under heavy shade with jars of water that had been frozen overnight, the big blocks of ice melted away almost to nothing. It was George who almost spoke first, but Kyle William's words rushed in as his father drew a breath.

"Mama really wants me to go to the altar. She seems scared that I ain't."

"Well, are you?" his father asked. "You're gittin old for it."

"You just got baptized. Don't seem like you can git too old for it."

"Well there's no use doin it unless you feel it. You just be getting up in front of those people and wasting your time and theirs if you don't."

"But that's just it," Kyle William said. "I'm scared I ain't never gonna feel it."

"You keep thinking like that and you never will. Didn't your grandfather teach you anything?"

George took a drink out of one of the jars. The water seemed to invade every part of his body the same way the darting water of the creek invaded every part of his brain.

"Why did you want to do it?" Kyle William asked.

His father sighed. The ice had melted in his jar. He wanted to pitch out what was left, but stopped himself. He was angry but he didn't know why. "I don't know what it is you're looking for from me. In the end you'll be your own judgment and that might be the hardest thing." He stood up and walked to where he'd left his hoe at the end of the row.

Kyle William got up and followed his father. He could see the muscles in the hard line of his father's jaw flickering. He thought of the old man's eyes filling with the river water and wondered what good there was in something that didn't change you. He felt he was sick with something that no one could understand. His grandfather was dead. His father was not really a holy man. His mother seemed to condemn him. He imagined the sickness to be similar to what had happened to his father in the river.

They worked on in silence and when they reached the end of the next row, his mother came out with bags of sandwiches and cool, salted cucumbers.

By the time their work was done at the end of the day, the light on the fields was bloody. The woods as the sun set turned to flat black rimmed with red and gold. Kyle William stared at the darkening plants until he could no longer make sense of them, until it seemed the molecules of the leaves were trading with the darkness of the shadows on the dirt. The early stars were bright, cold, and bloodless.

That night Kyle William silently closed the screen door after prayers and made his way to the woods at the edge of the fields. He heard his father's snoring out on the porch as he left. Kyle William stepped into the dark of the forest, ripping his pants on their neighbor's barbed wire cattle fence. He heard the small sounds of the animals within. The sounds grew louder and they made sense to him. He thought he could hear people that he did not fully understand talking, feel shoulders brushing against him as he walked deeper into the woods. Everything became darker and darker. The trees were obliterated. He could have been in a place like hell that did not burn and he would not have known. He felt he was very close to something that he might never be able to find. He heard the babbling of a small creek and was drawn to it. It was one of the few things he could see by the partially obscured moonlight. He dipped his hands in it and it was cold and fresh. A firefly glowed and disappeared and glowed near him. He decided that he must go back to the baptismal river alone.

The next evening after supper Kyle William went down to the river. He remembered the red clay and pouring sun from the day his father was baptized.

There was still a hint of clear blue in the sky. Familiar shadows crept out of the cool wood. Kyle William thought about taking off his shoes and letting the clay mud fill the spaces between his toes. He thought of his mother, father, and grandfather. He stripped off his shirt and watched it fall to the ground. It appeared almost luminous. He watched the many broiling red currents of the river and gathered up a handful of stones and skipped them halfway across it. He laughed quietly, the stones knocking back and forth against each other in his warm fist. The red mud sucked at his shoes, but he paid it no mind.

Tennessee Jones lives in Brooklyn, New York. His work has appeared in numerous publications, including *Lodestar Quarterly* and *LIT*. He is also the author of the zine *Teenage Death Songs*. He was raised in the mountains of East Tennessee.